Peter Hamilton Myers

**The first of the Knickerbockers**

A tale of 1673

Peter Hamilton Myers

**The first of the Knickerbockers**
*A tale of 1673*

ISBN/EAN: 9783337022860

Printed in Europe, USA, Canada, Australia, Japan

Cover: Foto ©Andreas Hilbeck / pixelio.de

More available books at **www.hansebooks.com**

# FIRST OF THE KNICKERBOCKERS:

## A TALE OF 1673.

BY

## P. HAMILTON MYERS, Esq.,

AUTHOR OF THE "KING OF THE HURONS," "PRISONER OF THE BORDER," "BELL
BRANDON," "WHITE SACHEM," ETC.

NEW YORK:

CHAPMAN & CO., 116 NASSAU STREET,

THE AMERICAN NEWS CO., GENERAL AGENTS, 119 AND
121 NASSAU STREET.

1866.

McCREA & MILLER, Stereotypers.

# PREFACE.

Much wit has been expended upon prefaces; and it has sometimes happened that a whole string of brilliants, constituting, perhaps, an author's chief stock in trade, has been ostentatiously displayed at the door, as it were, of his book, luring the unsuspecting reader within, only to find that the interior of the edifice had been despoiled to ornament the vestibule. Such introductions may be compared to a large fire, lighted at the mouth of a cavern, which serves only to reveal the darkness within. Their writers, if yet another metaphor may be allowed, are like clocks at meridian; they first strike twelve, and afterwards preserve a low and monotonous ticking.

A preface, indeed, is dangerous ground for an author to tread upon. It should be short, pithy, and to the point. It should hold out no false promises; and should explain to that very exacting tribunal, the reading community, and to their vigilant purveyors, the critics, the claims to notice of the work which it introduces. It should be unassuming, concise, lucid, and bold; with a slight odor of incense for the very capacious nostrils of the Public, and a sort of gentle "by your leave" flashing of genuine wit. Despairing of attaining such a standard, the author of the following tale has determined to write no preface; although, out of regard to precedent, he has affixed that name to what might more properly be termed a postscript. Like that ingenious jeweller, however, who recommended his washed tinsel, by asserting, in Yankee phraseology, that the *best* part of it was gold, he would simply say, that although the following work is a fiction, designed to illustrate a great many things, the best, or most important part of the incidents conforms, with reasonable fidelity, to our earliest colonial history.

Two editions of this Book, in Library style, were issued, many years ago, by G. P. PUTNAM, but the work has been long out of print. The present is the first cheap edition ever offered to the public.

NEW YORK, Sept., 1866.

# THE

# FIRST OF THE KNICKERBOCKERS:

## A TALE OF 1673.

---

## CHAPTER I.

THE intelligent reader does not need to be told that, two centuries ago, our great Metropolis, then in an embryo state, together with a vast background of nebulous territory, was the colonial appendage alternately of England and Holland, and but lightly valued by either.

But let it not lower thy honest pride, oh vaunted Empire State! to remember those earlier days, when, in the shuttlecock state of thy existence, thou wast bandied about from owner to owner, now seized by force, and now a mere make-weight, thrown in to settle some more important bargain. And thou, oh gorgeous city of Manhattan! mart of nations! blush not to own thy former self in a small provincial town, clustered around its parent fortress, to carry out the pleasing illusion of protection beneath its dread armament of sixteen frowning guns. Formidable at least were they to the prowling savage, lurking in undiscovered haunts, where now the tide of human life rolls thickest, and where loudest comes the busy hum of commerce to the ear.

Renowned among the primitive patriarchs of the New Netherlands, a stickler for the dignity and honor of the States General, and a fitting representative of his transatlantic progenitors, was old Evert Knickerbocker. His fortunes, like his affections, were so intimately connected with the rise and decadence of the ancient Dutch dynasty in New Amsterdam, as to render an account of the one to some extent a history of the other.

Yet to neither of these weighty tasks does the humble pen of the present narrator aspire. An outline sketch of the character and fortunes of the venerable Evert is all that can with safety be promised ; for the shades of his cotemporary heroes are also hovering near, and many thronging memories are summoned from the cloudy realms of Tradition, obedient to the spell of that magical name. To throw around these aerial messengers the fetters of pen and ink, and to preserve them a little longer from their destined oblivion, or mayhap, ah, wo is me! to hasten them, by an unfortunate association, to that gloomy end,—such is my more humble expectation. Thy memory, oh noble and magnanimous Evert! embodiment of the sterling virtues of a noble and magnanimous people, may form indeed the theme of passing eulogy, thy frailties perhaps elicit a passing smile. But thou art introduced now and here (be quiet, restive shade!) rather as the usher and forerunner of one claiming a more distinguished notice. Nay, never shake thy hoary locks at me! A friend and confidant of the valiant Stuyvesant, sayest thou ? a member of his privy council? one of his body-guard, as 'twere? What though thou wert? Thou art a shade, innocuous now, and must stand awhile aside, while Youth and Beauty claim our first regard.

Youth and Beauty! Perennial ideas of a flitting reality! how like the sunshine do ye glide from point to point, among the generations of men, gilding with your beams each successive race, and followed still by the penumbra of advancing age. Not such, however, are their reflections who bask within your beams, nor such were thine, oh pure and peerless Effie! fairest of Manhattan's many fair! rejoicing in thy dowry of charms, profuse as blossoms on the vernal bough. The shade of Evert stands appeased, and smiles approving now, willing, as in life, to concede to thee, sole centre of his love, all precedence of praise.

A picture of happiness and content were they, the gray-haired man and his beautiful daughter, sitting at summer's twilight in the open porch that overlooked the silvery Hudson, while fragrant wreaths of smoke hung suspended, halo-like, above the head of the one, and glossy curls, brown, rich, and silken, floated as airily around the gently-tinted cheeks of the other.

If shadows could make indentures, Evert's portrait would have adorned the wall, daguerreotyped by the setting sun ; for where now he sat had he regularly smoked his evening pipe, through the warm months of summer, for twenty-five long years. There, eight years before, had he been startled from his wonted reverie upon the future greatness of the New Netherlands, and the growing honor of their High Mightinesses, by the booming guns, whose echoes across the bay and through the distant forests were but the prolonged dirge of his patriotic hopes. An English fleet was in the harbor, and an English army on its decks. Not numerous, it is true, were the foe, nor many were their floating forts, but there was enough to strike terror into many an honest burgher's heart, and to turn the lips of Evert whiter than the falling ashes of his pipe.

Yes, the crowning calamity had come; the reverberations of the threatening cannon had died away; the lofty demand of surrendry, the patriotic resolves of the few, the pusillanimous capitulation of the many—all was over. The gallant governor was deposed, and Sir Richard Nichols reigned in his stead. But, saith an ancient and punning chronicler, unknown to the present age, if Nichols *reigned*, Stuyvesant *stormed*, and tempestuous indeed was the time.

And Evert, too, was at first turbulent with wrath; but in his milder nature that gusty passion soon sank to a subdued and gentle grief; and nightly, now, as he took his accustomed seat, did he lament the passing away of the good old times, and, with fragmentary hopes of their return, build airy castles, smoke-encircled, and vanishing in smoke. But time had tempered his grief, and moderated his expectations. A change *might* come—he would not despair; but he no longer looked daily to see the gallant Tromp whitening the Narrows with his crowded sails, nor watched the iron weather-cock for favoring winds to let in the imaginary fleet. With Stuyvesant, now a private citizen, and his boon companion, he revelled in the memories of the past, and enjoyed, not sparingly, the creature comforts of life, with a zest seemingly but little impaired by care.

But Evert had substantial cause for his attachment to the parent country. His large possessions—and very large they were—were chiefly the fruit of her bounty, a munificent requital for early colonial services which had been deemed important by the home government. His estate lay chiefly upon Long Island, although his homestead was in the city, and he held an unheeded title-deed for a few hundred acres of wild land a mile beyond the city wall, and stretching along the shore of the Hudson.

His household, at the period now spoken of, consisted only of himself and two children, with the usual retinue of slaves incident, even at that early day, to all the wealthy Dutch families. The beautiful Effie has already been named, and of her brother it is sufficient, at present, to say that he was a merry, rattling wag of twenty-two, full of life, and utterly indifferent, as long as he was allowed to pursue his piscatory and forest sports unmolested, whether Charles the Second was his sovereign, or whether he was under the dominion of their Mighty Highnesses (as he used to call them), the States General of Holland.

It will naturally be supposed that Effie, the beautiful, and the heiress, was not without her admirers; for our ancestors of that age, unlike ourselves, are said not always to have been indifferent to metallic charms. Suitors she certainly had, and while we have been wandering, instead, to other subjects, it ought to have been said that the party on the Dutch councillor's stoop had been increased to three—that a young and buckish-looking gallant was disputing with the kitten the honor of holding Miss Effie's ball of worsted, and that the little belle, smiling coldly, was listening with a semi-frown to the pretty flatteries of her companion.

## CHAPTER II.

Among the colleagues of the venerable Mr. Knickerbocker in the council-board of the last governor of New Netherlands, was one Wilhelmus Groesbeck, the counterpart in many respects of Evert, his co-immigrant in early life, and, as the latter was accustomed to designate him, a man of substance. But, alas, for time and change! the New Netherlands had ceased to exist; the governor no longer wielded the dread *baton* of office; the council-board was broken up, and the man of substance was a shade.

Although in life Wilhelmus had enjoyed the pleasing illusion of being the owner of a certain portion of the planet on which he had been permitted to live, his title, as grave men of the law advise, extending to the centre of the earth, three thousand nine hundred and sixty-seven miles (and some odd feet, which he was willing to throw off), notwithstanding all this, he died, it is believed, without materially changing the position of his property. Not, however, without decidedly changing the position of a scape-grace son, who had watched hopefully his progenitor's apoplectic symptoms for many years, and who was disconsolate indeed—until all attempts at resuscitation were abandoned. This son, by that strange perversity of affection so often observed, had ever been the chief object of his father's regard, and found himself now the principal heir to his estate, and the direct devisee of many wise and well-worded admonitions besides.

That Egbert was a *first* child, and thus peculiarly the remembrancer of one who had long forsaken earth—that he bore *her* features—that he had been *her* idol—these perhaps were some of the strands of that strong paternal affection which had outlived ingratitude and rebellion. For Wilhelmus had another son, who, if not disinherited, was left comparatively indigent, and dependent in part upon the bounty of his elder brother, to whose protection he was commended. The partial parent, proud of his estate, had been desirous that it should be preserved entire, in one branch of the family; and there was something in the bold and dashing air of his eldest boy which commended him to the father's view, as a fitting person to perpetuate the ancestral honors. He was a headlong fellow, and, although entirely selfish and unprincipled, bore an exterior of frankness and candor, not a little pleasing to the casual observer. He was a famous sportsman too, and had carried off the honors of the chase on many a well-contested field—triumphs so nearly martial, as to elevate him highly in the good graces of the late military governor.

Rudolph was bookish, mild, and contemplative. He soared to many an empyrean eminence of thought, and if he took any flying leaps, it was upon the winged steed of Parnassus. He never participated in the wassail or the song with the bloods of the day, the ebullitions of whose coarser nature seemed to jar upon his sensitive mind. Yet his heart was a well-spring of every noble affection, and he was alive to all the harmonies and beauties of Nature. If modest and retiring, he was firm and stable in his character (thanks to his Flemish blood!), and he was possessed of a fund of humor, which, although always sparkling, seldom degenerated into sarcasm. Such were the brothers, to whom the great Groesbeck estate had descended, in a shower of wealth to the one, and a slender competence to the other.

But Egbert had additional cause for self-gratulation, besides that of being the recipient of so bountiful a patrimony; for he was the affianced partner of the beautiful Effie. Not that any personal compact existed between them, but the matter had been arranged years before, by older heads, which, shaking themselves wisely together, had settled the whole affair, leaving nothing at all for the youngsters to do, excepting quietly to acquiesce in the proposed arrangement, when the set time should arrive.

What effect Egbert's sudden enfranchisement from paternal authority was like to have upon the matter, did not at once appear. Certain it is that he showed no proper appreciation of his privileges. The fruit which hangs within our grasp, however rich and luscious, is not always the most tempting; for the eye ever wanders to the more distant branches, and searches for inaccessible treasures. Indeed, the modest and retiring charms of Effie were scarcely calculated to captivate so coarse a mind as that of Egbert. The hoyden beauty who could meet midway his addresses, who could flatter and cajole him, who could talk vociferously and laugh boisterously, was far more likely to attract his admiration; and such a charmer, unfortunately for the young heir, lived in his neighborhood, the sole object of whose ambition was his subjugation.

She was the daughter of one Hiram Sharp, a man who had transferred his talents from one of the New England settlements to that of New York, but a few years prior to the period now spoken of. As this latter personage, like his daughter, is destined to figure somewhat in the following narrative, it may be allowable here briefly to describe him. Of Miss Euphemia, and of her younger brother, who was just arrived at man's estate, and rejoiced in the sonorous name of Benhadad, little need at present be said, as the progress of this history will sufficiently develope their prominent beauties of character. Hiram had been a lawyer, and one of that variety which so often brings opprobrium upon his noble profession. The organ of cunning, whatever may be its designation in the nomenclature of phrenology, was the nucleus of his brain : his pineal gland was there, and his soul; for Hiram was what is called an acute man. He was wide awake, as the saying is; that is to say, he was always looking out for his own interests, and looking on coldly, yet closely, at everything else. Of about fifty years, rather tall, slightly stooping, with a sharp spectacled face, and little restless gray eyes, laughing much, and sneering more, but always watching—such was Mr. Sharp.

He was not, at the time now spoken of, properly a lawyer, for he had abandoned his profession, and was engaged in a miscellaneous trading business far more lucrative. He bought peltry of the Indians, poor simpletons, who thronged his doors, eager to exchange the wealth of the forests for valueless trinkets, or the suicidal draught. He was suspected, too, of carrying on a still more reprehensible species of commerce. It is well known that, in that early state of the colony, the government, weak, and unsettled, was often compelled to wink at the greatest enormities. Pirates thronged the seas, and, scarcely dissembling their character, visited the settlements. They were, of course, a rough, bull-dog race, whose huge whiskers and jaunty caps were a terror to all beholders, and the weak officials of the law were fain to believe them good honest seamen, a little eccentric perhaps, but evidently industrious and thriving.

These worthies were often seen lounging about Hiram's store, and if rich foreign fabrics adorned his shelves more plentifully on such occasions—it was a coincidence certainly, but what was a coincidence! You would not deprive a man of his good name merely on suspicion, gentle reader, and if you would, let me tell you that your ancestors were far more charitable. Certain it is that Hiram Sharp was famed for being a man of good moral character. It was what he prided himself upon. He could have brought troops of witnesses to any tribunal to testify to it, and Captain Ripley, the gentleman from Portugal, would have clinched the matter with more oaths, probably, than any magistrate would have required.

It is scarcely necessary to say that Mr. Sharp waxed wealthy.

His roots struck deep into the soil, and his branches overshadowed the land.  They overshadowed, too, many an honest Dutch
burgher, who, in the quiet contemplation of his cabbages, his
pipes, and his chubby-headed boys, saw the tide of trade roll
turbulently by, without ever dreaming of embarking upon its
treacherous surface.  They vented some harmless imprecations,
at times, upon the upstart Yankee, fully believing that Satan was
his right-hand man, and that he would yet be seen flying away
bodily with the wily lawyer and all his ill-gotten treasures.

Mr. Knickerbocker was among the few wealthy Hollanders
whose possessions greatly exceeded those of the New Englander,
and the stock of moral qualities which was hoarded up in the guileless breast of the latter was enhanced and beautified by the crowning one of envy.  He could not bear to see the silver-haired Evert
walking quietly about, with his hands behind him, the acknowledged proprietor of fifty thousand acres of land.  And when he
learned that his own amiable daughter, imbued with paternal prudence, was angling wilily for the treasures of the defunct Groesbeck,
his dislike to the Knickerbockers was by no means diminished;
for he knew well the intended union of Egbert and Effie, and
he had but little hope that it could be prevented.

But when Hiram could do nothing else, he could *watch*, and
silently and calmly he observed the course of events.  Yet, vigilant as he was, there were some things which eluded his observation, or he would have ceased so eagerly to desire the alliance
which he contemplated for his daughter.  Egbert's wealth gave
but little promise of perpetuity.  A career marked by folly and
extravagance did not necessarily lead him to transcend his ample
income; but there is one variety of vice which undermines with
facility the most colossal fortunes.  If the administration of the
Duke of York had been signalized by a large accession of English
gentry and gallant cavaliers to the province, it had also been
marked by the influx of adventurers of every description.  Gam-
bling had then as now its fashionable devotees, and its systematic
sharpers, who were quick to discover their legitimate prey; and
when it is said that Egbert unwarily ventured within the circuit
of this great moral maelstrom, the precariousness of his possessions will be readily conceded.  But his addiction to so fatal a
habit, notwithstanding his losses had already been large, was
unknown even to the astute Hiram, and was of course unsus-
pected by Mr. Knickerbocker; for the heavy mortgages which
lay upon his fair fields did not change their smiling aspect, or
check their growing verdure.

Long wavering in his choice between the lawyer's daughter
and the gentle Effie, it was only by views of a mercenary character that he was at length brought to a decision, and foregoing

his frequent visits to the former, he seemed to prosecute with earnestness his claims upon his affianced bride.   Now Effie had a heart full of all pure and noble emotions, and in her utter loneliness would doubtless easily have been won by a generous and worthy wooer.   But she had been offended by Egbert's seeming indifference, and resolved, with true feminine spirit, to punish him, if only with temporary resentment.   Well would it have been for the tardy lover if the gentle vengeance of Effie had been all that he had to dread.

## CHAPTER III.

WELL might the venerable Evert look regretfully back upon departed days of Dutch dominion in the province of the New Netherlands. So many were the invidious distinctions made between the Dutch and English residents, by the new authorities, and so needless the vexation and disquiet inflicted upon the former, that some began to take alarm, lest even the titles to real estate which had been acquired under the old dynasty should be set aside. The power bestowed by the Duke of York upon Governors Nichols and Lovelace was of a plenary nature, and was executed much in accordance with the despotic spirit which, at that period, marked the British rule.

If, however, Governor Lovelace looked with an evil eye upon some of the more wealthy Hollanders, he did not attempt to dispossess them of their lands, but, following the example of Sir Richard Nichols, he reaped a rich harvest of fees, by requiring a renewal of all patents which had been granted by the former government. The brief administration of his predecessor had left his labor unaccomplished, and even Lovelace probably consulted the exigencies of his private exchequer, in the time and manner of enforcing the requirement. But early in the autumn of the year 1672, the few who had neglected previous admonitions on this point were warned, by a governmental edict, of the necessity of compliance within a prescribed period.

Among those by whom this mandate had hitherto been unheeded, and who now prepared to give it a grumbling acquiescence, was Mr. Knickerbocker; but what was his consternation on being unable, after the most diligent search, to find any trace of a patent for his own extensive domains. In vain was the depository of family writings ransacked, and countless old papers, musty and mildewed, brought to light. Bending over chests, rummaging through drawers, reaching to topmost shelves, and peering into dark corners, the alarmed old man passed a whole day, without success. Tired with his labor, he sat down to reflect, and although he distinctly remembered that his manor rights had been settled in council, fifteen years before, and that he was then fully entitled to his patent, he could not recall to mind the existence of any such instrument. He did not remember ever to have seen it, and the fearful truth gradually forced itself upon his mind, that by some strange oversight it never had been executed. A blind confidence in the stability of the then existing government was doubtless, in some degree, the cause of this culpable negligence.

But how dreadful was his dilemma! Watchful enemies on every side, and so strong a pretext for wresting his estate from his hands. He knew full well that, if he had no deed, his lands would be regarded as having belonged to the Dutch government at the time of the conquest, and as having passed, by that event, to the new sovereignty. Desperate with fear, he resumed his laborious search, and quitted it only when exhausted both in body and mind. On the next day he gained access to the public office where the object of his search, if in existence, should have been recorded, and, without disclosing his object to any, made a diligent examination, which proved equally fruitless. It is needless to say that he returned to his home a sad and dispirited man. All his vast possessions seemed slipping from his grasp, as it were by some necromantic wile.

It was a consolation, however, to reflect that as yet he was the sole possessor of this important secret; and, earnestly hoping that what had so long remained undiscovered might continue to be concealed, he resolved to maintain a perfect silence upon the subject. Doubtless, he thought, the new instrument could be constructed without any reference to the old, for the tract to be embraced in it was known as certain distinct townships, and required no definite description. Such was the judicious reasoning of Evert, but reason and resolution did not allay his alarm. With the mania of a mind filled with a single idea, he was haunted day and night by the dreadful fear that some accident would betray the momentous truth.

Quietude became a stranger to his breast, and sleep forsook his pillow; or else even in dreams his grief returned. Visionary sheriffs surrounded his bed, serving countless writs of ejectment: long parchment processes, the very caligraphy of which was fierce and threatening, unrolled themselves before his eyes: little mocking demons perched upon his bed-posts, and, grinning widely, whispered to each other, "*He hasn't any title!*" and one, bending even over his pillow, with cheeks distended like a trumpeter's, shouted into his ears, "*Where's your patent? Where's your patent?*"

Morning came, and he walked about his grounds for relief; but fear and suspicion were his companions. The very fowls seemed to be cackling forth his secret. Chanticleer jumped upon the fence, and crowed it to the winds; the ducks were babbling about it in the pond; the geese, with long necks outstretched, hissed it in his ears; and a fierce old gobbler, his gills red with wrath, eyed him askance, as he sputtered forth his views on the subject, with wonderful volubility, though fortunately in an unknown tongue.

He strolled into the city, and sought diversion of mind. His walk led him directly past the store of the attorney, whose meddling propensities he was well acquainted with, and whom, of all men, he dreaded most to encounter. He was just congratulating himself on getting past unaccosted, when the sharp visage and sharper voice of the lawyer made him cognizant of his approach. Evert prepared to give him a civil good day, and glide quietly by, but the other evidently contemplated some further salutation. He had a pencil in one hand, and in the other a little scrap of paper, scrawled all over with figures and diagrams, and there was an ominous pen behind his ear; altogether, never had the lawyer looked so formidable. He came up close to Evert, and poked his sharp nose almost into the old man's face, as, with an awfully distinct articulation upon each word, he said,

"Mr. Knickerbocker, *where's—your—patent?*"

Poor Evert's heart stood still; the blood forsook his face, and the showering ashes fell, flake-like, from his trembling pipe. Several seconds elapsed before he could reply, and the lawyer, who in reality designed nothing more than to elucidate some trifling boundary question, stood wondering at his emotion. Now, great as was Evert's alarm, he would not, in the singleness of his heart, have uttered a wilful falsehood for his whole estate, and he replied, stammeringly, that he did not think he could lay his hand upon it at that moment.

"Oh, of course not," said Hiram. "I did not suppose that you carried it about with you, but I wanted to know how far north your ridge farm extends, as I have a tract of land adjoining;" and the lawyer went on, chattering about links, and chains, and blazed trees, and stakes, and stones, and surveyors, until all these ideas were floating in a complete whirl through the brain of his bewildered auditor. Evert inquired what boundary Mr. Sharp claimed upon the south, and upon the latter designating one which clearly embraced a few acres of his own land, he replied,

"Very well, Mr. Sharp, I'll not dispute it with you; put your fence where *you* think the line is, and it shall be all right."

The lawyer, gratified and astonished, bowed in reply; but, as Evert was walking off, he gave him the gratifying assurance that he would walk over to his house, nevertheless, on some fine day, and *look at the patent*—as he wanted to see about the

Whiston and Pebble Bay tracts, and about the Cove—and about——

"Yes—yes—yes," said the old man, tearing himself away, with sad forebodings, "any time—any time. You'll come soon enough," he muttered to himself—"it's all gone: I see it clearly now, it's all gone—ah! my poor, poor Effie."

Evert went home utterly appalled. Ruin was staring him in the face, pulling him by the sleeve, pushing him from behind, surrounding him on every side. Sharp would certainly come. Nothing in the world could stop him. An avalanche would not have been a feather in his path—an earthquake might have shaken *him*, but not his purpose. He could not fail to discover the whole secret, for the absence of the patent would arouse all his suspicions, and set his infernal wits at work. Thus thought the ex-councillor, and not without reason. From the moment when he parted with the wily lawyer, the latter had not ceased to wonder at his singular emotion. Malice sharpened his wits, and his suspicions soon taking the right direction, he flew to the colonial record office, and to his unspeakable delight found that it contained no trace of Evert's title.

His doubts now became certainty—the agitation of the old man was all accounted for, and Hiram rubbed his hands, and grinned gleefully, as he thought how many desirable objects the discovery of this momentous secret would enable him to accomplish. It was true, the recording of the patent was not essential to its validity, and, if Evert could produce it, his rights could not be questioned; but that he could not do so seemed nearly certain. Why else should it remain absent from the public books, 'and why such unnecessary alarm? The patent was either lost, or had never been executed, and, in either case, Hiram foresaw the downfall of his rival, a bountiful slice of his manor in his own hands, as a reward for his fidelity to the state, and above all, a probable recovery of the mercenary Groesbeck and his extensive estates.

With such inducements for effort, he resolved to leave nothing undone; and, suspending all other labors, he gave his mind solely to this magnanimous enterprise. His first step was to call upon Governor Lovelace, with whom he had long been on confidential terms, and whose favor and powerful patronage rendered him additionally formidable. He did not, however, fully disclose his errand to that functionary at first, but only hinted in general terms at his important secret, seeking to elicit the views and feelings of his companion. Lovelace, however, was not a man to be trifled with, and perceiving, more by the lawyer's countenance and manner, than by his words, that his mind was teeming with some important matter, he hastily replied:—

"Speak out, Mr. Sharp, speak out—you talk of escheats, and forfeitures, and rewards quite too blindly. Tell your whole story, sir; it is no small game that you have treed, I'll be sworn, and if it is any of these smoke-dried, disloyal old curmudgeons who go about with their gold-headed canes, prating of their High Mightinesses, the States General, you may name your own price, sir, your own price, within the bounds of reason."

"Would a fifth be too much?" suggested Sharp, nervously.

"A fifth, Hiram? why, you grow modest, man—you do indeed—you shall have a *third*, sir, a *third*," returned Lovelace, who had, in reality, but little idea of the magnitude of the lawyer's "game." Sharp now eagerly disclosed his whole story, to the great surprise of his companion, and the conference that followed was long and confidential. Let it suffice that, when Hiram went home, he was in a flush of excitement and joy, and he resolved to call on Mr. Knickerbocker the very next day, and request a view of the patent.

## CHAPTER IV.

OVERWHELMED with the fear of his impending calamity, Evert in the meantime resolved to apply to his old friend, Governor Stuyvesant, for advice. The thought relieved him, and he flew to put it into execution. The ex-governor, who had retired from the city at the time of the conquest by the English, resided about two miles north of the wall, on his farm or *Bowerie*, a locality as far within the bounds of the modern town as it was beyond the precincts of the old.

He received Evert's intelligence in silence, and listened to the thrice-repeated story of the garrulous old man without reply. His countenance gave no indication of his thoughts, but his friend could read his changing emotions with sufficient accuracy, in the varying puffs that escaped from his pipe. The dense, dark cloud which burst forth at first, the little angry puffs that succeeded, and the light, easy, graceful wreaths that next ensued, were all intelligible. There was surprise and alarm at the danger—contemptuous indignation at the lawyer, and, finally, distinct and certain relief. Poor Evert's eye brightened as he beheld these harbingers of hope floating gracefully over his companion's head. He seized the hand of his friend, and, with watery eyes, looked the gratitude of his heart. Stuyvesant smiled in reply, and, lowering his pipe for the first time, he said :

"Go home, Mr. Knickerbocker, and be quiet ; *I think I know where your patent is.* Hans shall bring it to you. Go home, and go to bed, for you look like a *spook*, Mr. Knickerbocker— go home, go home," he continued, shaking the old man's hand, and holding him fast the meanwhile ; and then, his whole face changing to a thundercloud, he sputtered forth a string of Dutch anathemas at the meddling lawyer, as he turned hastily away, and left Evert quietly to pursue his homeward path.

Hans, a tub-like lad of eighteen, was called and despatched at once to summon to the governor's presence Mynheer Teunis Vanderbilt, an old, spare, spindle-shanked, shadowy man, scarcely larger than the smallest of his own money-bags, who had at one time been chief officer of state under the valiant

Stuyvesant. He had been a sort of prime minister, chief councillor, civic and military secretary, and aid-de-camp, acting also
occasionally as envoy extraordinary to Yankeedom and New
Sweden. In these capacities and others, he had not only contrived to feather his own nest pretty effectually, but had treas-
ured up a wholesome degree of wrath against the Yankees, and,
like Stuyvesant, he now watched with jealous eyes all encroach-
ments upon the privileges of his order, the old aristocracy of
the land.

When Mr. Vanderbilt arrived at the house of his friend, he
found the latter sitting beside a table, on which were writing
materials, and a large blank sheet of parchment. There was a
vacant chair at the board, of which Teunis took possession, and
lighting his pipe, a silent fumigation ensued for about half an
hour, the secretary's eye falling occasionally with an inquiring
glance upon the parchment.

" Hef you forgotten how to write, Teunis?" at length inquired
the governor, between puffs.

"Nain—nain, Mynheer," replied the secretary, laughing, "Ich
can write *my name*."

"I don't believe it," returned Stuyvesant, quietly.

Teunis gravely repeated his assertion. It was indeed a lesson
that he had taken too much pains to learn, to allow of his easily
forgetting it, for the sum total of his chirographical education
had been devoted to the acquirement of that one accomplishment, the art of writing *his name*. The force of learning could
no further go.

Stuyvesant pushed the parchment toward his amazed companion, and, putting a pen into his hand, pointed to the lower
left-hand corner of the sheet. Amazement seized upon poor
Teunis, who stared first at the parchment, and then at the governor ; but the latter, with his eyes fixed upon the ceiling, sat
puffing a regular ha! ha! and seemed utterly unconscious of his
presence. The secretary seized the pen, and, after some ineffectual attempts to mend it with his tobacco knife, set himself about
his task. It was a tedious job, and the little man paused after ac-
complishing the first half, and smoked a pipe before resuming his
labors, eyeing meanwhile, with much complacency, the scrawl
before him, which might easily have been mistaken for the portrait of a many-legged spider. At last, however, the feat was
satisfactorily performed, and Stuyvesant owned himself mistaken.

Mynheer Vanderbilt, however, was an astute man, and, after
much silent cogitation, he began to wonder what was in the
wind ; but his old habits of deference to his superior prevented
him from encroaching upon his confidence by inquiring into

anything which the other seemed desirous to conceal. He, therefore, rose to depart, and was arrested for a moment in the doorway by the voice of his friend.

"Teunis!" said the governor, gruffly.

The secretary turned, and looked back.

"Teunis!" repeated Stuyvesant, more emphatically.

"Wal, Mynheer!" was the response.

The governor laid down his pipe, and pressed his forefinger upon his closed lips, until the displaced blood left them as colorless as the wall. Vanderbilt replied to this pantomime by a similar gesture, and departed.

No sooner was Stuyvesant left alone, than he seemed desirous of ascertaining whether he also retained the art of writing, and taking the pen which lay beside him, he affixed his own name to the lower right-hand corner of the parchment, opposite that of the secretary. This being done, the services of Hans were once more in requisition. Again he went into the city, and returned this time accompanied by another elderly man, whose sagacious look, and quick rolling eye, gave token of a different order of intellect. He was, in fact, an ancient Dutch lawyer, who stood high in the confidence of the governor, and whose little crotchety handwriting was to be seen on all the public documents of the late administration.

But, like many other sagacious men, Mynheer Myndert Ten Eyck had contrived to overlook the main chance, and had found himself, in the downhill of life, almost a pensioner upon the bounty of his ancient comrades. He had no reason, however, to complain of stinted generosity on the part of the ex-governor, and it was owing perhaps partly to this circumstance that he had responded with such alacrity to the summons of the latter. Stuyvesant had arranged a chair for him at the table in such a manner that he could scarcely fail to observe the mysterious parchment, with its signatures in blank; but this precaution was quite unnecessary, for Mynheer Ten Eyck would have discovered it, had it lain in the darkest corner of the room. The governor proceeded at once to business, by informing his visitor of Mr. Knickerbocker's loss, and of the immense importance of finding the document without delay.

"I have reason to think," he said, "that it is in your possession, Mr. Ten Eyck, inasmuch as you wrote all the old patents, and I want you *to look for it*, and *to look very sharp*,"—and again his merry pipe sent forth a succession of little laughing puffs, while the gravity of his countenance remained undisturbed.

The lawyer comprehended the whole subject; that he did so was sufficiently evident from the fact, that while his companion was looking another way, he had already slipped the parchment slyly into his pocket. "I think I can find Mr. Knickerbocker's patent," he replied; but a cloud of doubt rested on his face, as he slowly continued, "but I hope you have considered——"

"Everything," retorted the governor, angrily. "I have considered everything, Mr. Ten Eyck, and it must be *found*. I will be responsible—*I, sir*—Peter Stuyvesant, with my manors and estates. Do you understand me *now?*"

The lawyer bowed.

"Donner and blitzen!" exclaimed the old man, striding up and down the room till the house echoed with the strokes of his wooden leg upon the oaken floor—"Donner and blitzen!" he said, scowling at the frightened attorney, "would you sit still and see the finest estate in the province confiscated, and the gray-haired Evert in the poor-house, while a parcel of idle Yankees were rioting on his lands? Would you——"

How far the venerable Peter's oration would have extended is uncertain, but on the breaking away of a thick cloud, which had hung stationary for some time, midway to the ceiling, he discovered that his auditor was missing.

Scarce two hours had elapsed, however, before a messenger from the attorney arrived, who delivered a sealed package into the hands of Mr. Stuyvesant, and disappeared. The latter eagerly tore off the envelope, and, to his great amazement, beheld an old, worn, smoke-dried, mouse-nibbled sheet of parchment, containing letters patent to Evert Knickerbocker for all his manor lands. It was dated in 1657—bore the signatures of Peter Stuyvesant as governor, and Teunis Vanderbilt as secretary, and had an old dirty seal of white wax appended to it with a faded blue ribbon. Again and again did the governor examine and scrutinize it with the most overwhelming astonishment.

"The tuyfel is in the lawyer," he exclaimed at length, after turning it over for the fiftieth time; and had it not been for an extra cross which he had accidentally bestowed upon the final letter of his name, he would have sworn that the document before him was in every respect genuine. As it was, his delight knew no bounds. Calling upon Hans once more, he despatched him with the precious document, carefully enveloped, to Mr. Knickerbocker, whose amazement and joy had well-nigh overturned his reason; for no faintest gleam of suspicion did he entertain as to the authenticity of the deed. Soft was his pillow on that happy night; no spectral sheriffs were about it; the demons were all gone; and the long, spectacle-stridden nose and rat-gray eyes of Hiram Sharp did not peer from behind the bed-post once during the live-long night.

## CHAPTER V.

THE gray twilight of the ensuing morning saw the vigilant lawyer on his feet. Far different had been his repose from that of the venerable Evert, for all night long the clink of the surveyor's chain had been sounding in his ears, and little dancing figures, indicative of interminable distances, had floated before his eyes. Longitudinally, transversely, and diagonally, had he divided the Knickerbocker manor, and at every trial his own third part had proved, by some strange hocus pocus, larger than all the remainder.

He laughed at the remembrance of his dreams, but he looked on them as a good omen, and bestirred himself diligently at his labors. It was nearly mid-day, however, when he started on his important errand, for he was certain of then finding Evert at home, smoking his after-dinner pipe, in one corner of his long Dutch stoop. Despite his bountiful supply of brass, he was a little embarrassed at first, as he approached his supposed victim, and he attempted to hide his confusion by rapid talking.

"Good marnin', Mr. Knickerbocker, heow do you dew—I've called over about that air patent of yourn—jest want to look at it a minute—fine marnin'. You've been to dinner a'ready, hay? You Dutch people have dinner dreadful arly."

He had rattled on thus far, closely watching, meanwhile, the countenance of Evert, and he stopped now in surprise at the perfect equanimity of the latter, who, handing a seat to his visitor, called to Effie to bring the desired document. Puzzled beyond expression at these appearances, and not a little alarmed, Sharp was arguing to himself the impossibility of its being produced, when Effie came dancing out, and placed the sallow old parchment in his hands. Opening it, with an eager and wolf-like gaze, his eye ran rapidly across the sheet, and a feeling of utter discomfiture came over him. If it had been his own death-warrant he could scarcely have viewed it with more surprise and grief.

Again and again did he scan it, but, forced at length to admit to himself that there was no flaw in the instrument, he slowly folded it up, and was about returning it to Evert, when a sudden

2*

thought seemed to occur to him, and he drew back his hand. The remembrance of his recent conviction that the patent was not in existence, and the evidence which had sustained his belief, came back to his mind with such overwhelming force, that he resolved to make still another examination. For ten long minutes did he slowly inspect the paper, until every fold and stain and mark had been perused and re-perused, without success. Suddenly raising it, however, to the light, and looking through it, a glare of fiendish exultation shot across his features; for the faintly stamped mark of the manufacturers had caught his eye, revealing the dreadful figures "1671"!

"It is a forgery," he shouted; "a forgery!" holding it up before Evert, and pointing to the fearful proof, while the parchment shook and rattled in his unsteady hand, like an aspen in the breeze. A deathly pallor overspread the face of the old man: he rose tottering to his feet, gazed for a moment at the fatal figures, and then sank exhausted to his chair, with a despairing conviction that all was lost. A moments reflection convinced the wily lawyer of the true state of things. He knew that the signatures were both genuine, and he was equally well acquainted with the writing of Ten Eyck. That these three old cronies of Evert should have thus combined to help him out of a scrape, was the most natural thing in the world. But he knew also that Stuyvesant was at the bottom of the whole intrigue, and he would as willingly have encountered the arch-fiend as have got into a broil with the irate old governor.

His policy, therefore, was to profess to believe poor Ten Eyck the sole artificer of the patent, and that the names of Stuyvesant and Vanderbilt were counterfeited. He hastened, too, to bring about an *exposé* of the affair, lest the ex-governor might in some way outwit him after all. Taking advantage therefore of Evert's emotion, he slipped the patent into his pocket and departed. He bent his steps directly to the residence of Governor Lovelace, and, after a short interview with that officer, hastened to the house of Ten Eyck. The sight of Sharp with the open patent in his hand, a sudden accusation, and an appeal to the mischievous figures, overwhelmed the old man, and he could not reply. Hiram laid the parchment on the table, and paced the room as he conversed. There was a fire on the hearth, and his alarmed companion, taking advantage of a moment when the back of his accuser was turned to him, seized the evidence of his supposed crime and cast it into the flames. It was what Sharp had expected and desired. The fatal mischief was accomplished, and Evert Knickerbocker was a pauper.

Not in the literal sense of the word, yet reduced to the slender competence which the possession of a small homestead, and a few hundred pounds beside, might afford. In vain was every effort made to stay the operation of the dreadful machinery of the law; for Evert's rights were not surrendered without a vigorous effort for their retention. As to Sharp, the informer, enriched by his own infamy, his name would doubtless have become a reproach, had he not immediately set up a carriage, doubled his subscription to the minister, and talked largely about reforms, and all imaginable kinds of charities.

But the proper course of this narrative now carries us back to a time cotemporary with its opening scenes, and to the contemplation of other characters and different events.

## CHAPTER VI.

THE surprise and indignation of Rudolph Groesbeck at finding himself divested of his expected patrimony were not slight, and for a while he had entertained the illusive hope that his brother would rectify so apparent an injustice. But it soon became evident that Egbert contemplated no such unnecessary generosity. With the vanity of a little mind, he exulted over a brother whose superiority he had ever been compelled secretly to acknowledge; though it was rather Rudolph's elegance of person, and a certain intuitive grace of manner, which awakened his envy, than the advantages, less appreciable to him, of an enlarged mind, and a good education.

Rudolph was tall and well formed, and his face, radiant with intellectual light, possessed beauty of a higher order than any which mere symmetry of features can impart. Possessed of a scanty income, he found himself restricted to a quiet and obscure life, and subject, moreover, to the not infrequent taunts of Egbert, and his roystering companions, as a tame and spiritless fellow, destined to mope for a life-time among musty books. And such, at times, he fancied himself to be, secluded, owl-like, from the world, shutting his eyes to the daylight of the Present, and groping in the dim night of the Past. His owlship, however, was destined to be disturbed by the flittings of a butterfly. He met the beautiful Effie—each unknown to the other—rendered her some trifling courtesy, and returned to his books to find her sunny features upon every page, and to hear the melody of that one remembered tone outsounding all the grave voices of Antiquity.

The transforming power of Love has been the theme of all ages; and that it wrought its usual marvels upon Rudolph need not be doubted. His well-thumbed books were allowed a long respite upon their shelves, and he sought in frequent walks to encounter once more his unknown charmer. His poetic fancy had invested the very spot in which they had met with unwonted beauty, and its echoes seemed still vocal with the harmonies of her voice. He forgot his own poverty; he forgot, indeed, that there were such things as Wealth and Want. A rich and ex haustless mine of bliss seemed opened in his heart, which would prove triumphant over the ills of life, and independent of the vicissitudes of Time.

That Rudolph did not recognize the daughter of his father's chosen friend, whom as a child he had intimately known, is seemingly a matter of surprise. But Time, good old fellow, to give him his due, is not perpetually wielding his scythe to depopulate nations, or stooping with hammer and chisel at the base of mighty edifices, or changing the channels of rivers, or upbuilding islands in mid-ocean. For he had found leisure, during Rudolph's retirement, to develope so many beauties and graces in the gentle Effie, as to bury beneath their profusion her former self. So sinks the vase from view, concealed by bending flowers.

But it was no pleasure to the student to learn that his fair unknown was the daughter of the wealthy Evert. For a while, indeed, he wilfully closed his eyes to the disparity of fortune between them, and meeting her again and again, by a design which seemed like accident, he contrived to fasten more firmly the rosy fetters which enthralled him. Innocent of every art, and utterly unconscious of Rudolph's sentiments, Effie's genuine good nature and childish hilarity of spirits were unchecked in his presence by the reserve which might otherwise have detracted from her charms; and the lover soon found himself in the plight of the dazzled insect, which, unwarned by the singeing of its wings, continues to tempt Fate, until it rushes bodily into the flame. But the reflection which is not allowed to precede, is sure to follow our imprudent acts. Rudolph's dream of bliss was as brief as it was bright; for dismay seized upon his heart as he at length began to contemplate the gulf that intervened between himself and Effie.

The cold stage of his disease set in, and he flew to his books for relief. Homer paraded his Helens and Penelopes before him, and hinted at all the ruin they had wrought; Virgil dwelt complacently upon the charms of the magnificent Dido; Horace cracked a few unfeeling jokes on the subject of Love in general; Ovid offered to instruct him in the art; and Seneca, the grave old wag, buried to his chin in gold, descanted sagely upon the blessings of Poverty. Miserable comforters are ye all, thought the hapless Rudolph, as, turning his back upon his study, he strolled into the fields.

His sudden despair, however, had not been caused, or scarcely enhanced, by the existing engagement between Egbert and Effie, for to that event, while it remained unratified by any personal contract, he attached no manner of importance. It was

the grim spectre of Poverty, more formidable than the fabled
genii of the East, which stood scowling between him and the
bright Paradise of his hopes. Musing painfully upon his adverse
fortunes, he sauntered to the river, and, arranging the sails of a
small boat which he kept for pleasure excursions, embarked upon
the glassy tide.

It was a warm autumnal day, and the whole face of Nature
was wrapt in smiles. The sky was bright and blue above him,
and its image bright and blue below, and his white-winged bark
seemed suspended in mid-ether, floating cloud-like and buoyantly
along. The sportive sea-gulls were flitting around him, now
darting into the stream, and now flashing the sunlight from their
dripping wings, as they wheeled rapidly away. The trill of
many birds came faintly from the shore; the distant lowing of
cattle was heard, and the far-off voice of Chanticleer, the challenge and reply, at once disturbed and illustrated the silence of
the scene.

Rudolph's boat seemed instinctively to shape its course in the
direction of the Knickerbocker homestead, which stood on a
slight eminence, that sloped by a gentle declivity to the river.
At the bottom of the garden and on the very margin of the
stream was a latticed summer-house, clothed with flowering
vines, in which he loved to fancy the beautiful Effie, lulled to
repose by the silvery voice of the tiny billows at her feet.
Loosening his snowy sails opposite this sacred retreat, he loi-
tered midway of the stream, forgetting for a while his grief, and
wrapt in those bright dreams of the imagination, whose pris-
matic hues so often lend their radiance to the young and ingenuous mind.

Unheard was the shout of triumph which came ever and anon
from the fisherman's shallop, anchored in the distance, and the
louder detonation of the sportsman's gun, echoing among the
adjacent forests, disturbed not his reverie. His mind was revel-
ling in Elysian fields, for Hope, like the coral architect of the
sea, was rearing her gorgeous structures beneath the very billows of Despair. Thus feeding the fire that consumed him, the
hapless Rudolph gave way to the impulses of a generous and
guileless heart. The day waned, and he retired to his lonely
home, depressed by the re-action of his thoughts, his devotion
and his vigils unrewarded, even so much as by the fluttering of
a scarf in the breeze.

The time now spoken of was just that period when Egbert,
after a succession of heavy losses at the gaming table, began to
grow certain of his own affection for the beautiful heiress. His
marked addresses to Effie soon became generally known, and
Rudolph, smitten to the heart with his own adverse fate, resolved

to abandon a home darkened by so many griefs. In the settlement about Fort Orange, or, as it was called by the English, Fort Albany, resided a brother of the deceased Wilhelmus, whose often urged entreaties for a visit from Rudolph the latter now resolved to accept.

A sloop was preparing to sail for the fort, for the transmission of some munitions of war, and other government stores, to the garrisons at that settlement and at Schenectady. On board this vessel Rudolph embarked. The voyage was unusually long. There were head winds, and side winds, and no winds, to baffle the wary skipper, and there were stoppings at night, and safe anchorings to be found, and watchings for the day. Formal soundings too were to be made, even where the bottom was visible through the shallow and pellucid wave; and the coast was to be examined for future conquest; and the charcoal chart of Captain Van Dam was to be corrected by striking out three cannibal islands erroneously set down on a former voyage, and by inserting a volcanic mountain among the Highlands, which, like the pipe of its sage discoverer, is supposed to have long since burnt out. A week indeed elapsed before they had doubled St. Anthony's Nose, and another ere the six frowning guns of Fort Albany were visible. It mattered little, however, to Rudolph. He had his books and his *meerschaum*, and in the black-letter page of the one, and from the fragrant wreaths of the other, gleamed the radiant features which were at once the cause and the solace of his grief.

It was during his sojourn in these hyperborean regions that the important events recorded in the preceding chapters had occurred, of which no intelligence had yet crossed that mighty interval which stretched between the city of New York and the far northern outpost of Albany.

Egbert's wooing, meanwhile, had for a time given token of success, for Effie had unfortunately been accustomed to regard the alliance as a matter of duty. Her heart indeed was unwon, but then she knew nothing of the wealth of affection which lay dormant within it.

But the sudden calamity which had overwhelmed the house of the Knickerbockers, singularly enough, put a new aspect upon the snitor's zeal. The culminating point of his love seemed suddenly to be past, for the silvery voice of Effie, and her golden locks, like the bills of a broken bank, no longer represented the chink of the genuine coin. He had manifested much alarm at the first intimation of Mr. Knickerbocker's troubles, and for a while took an active part in attempting to defeat the machinations of Sharp. He esteemed himself, however, most fortunate in not having yet passed the Rubicon of proposal and acceptance, and resolved, while the peril impended, to maintain a middle ground between courtship and estrangement, from which it would be equally easy to advance or retreat.

Miss Sharp, in the meantime, did not cease to ply her artillery with great effect, whenever the enemy came within the range of her charms. She affected much commiseration for the Knicker-bockers, and regretted that the government should have employed her father in so unpleasant a duty as that of prosecuting its claims against him. She herself could bear witness to the sleepless nights which it had occasioned poor papa; and then her own feelings, to say nothing of Benhadad's, had been lacerated to an extent that it was really quite painful to mention. Such was the substance of Miss Euphemia's sentiments as detailed to Egbert, with as much of a languishing air as a pair of small, black eyes, and a mouth with a decidedly snap-dragonish expression, would admit of. But her fears and suspense were not of very long con-tinuance, for the news of the ultimate rejection of Evert's claims was speedily followed by another marked change in the deport-ment of Egbert. His attentions to Effie grew "small by degrees and beautifully less," and within a few weeks were altogether discontinued.

Poor old Evert, in all his troubles, had thought less of himself than of his children, and he consoled himself often by reflecting how well his darling Effie was provided for, and by hoping that Egbert, in the plenitude of his wealth and kindness, might possi-bly lend a helping hand also to his heedless son. It was with bitter grief and indignation, therefore, that he had discovered the perfidy of the heartless youth, nor would he indeed give any cre-dence to the signs of his desertion until compelled so to do. Far different, however, were Effie's feelings. A sense of relief, and of freedom from some hidden danger, gave new bloom to her face and fresh buoyancy to her steps. She grieved indeed for her father's sorrow, and sought ever to console him by the assurance that they would still do well enough.

"Remember," she would say, as she brushed the thin locks from his temples—"Remember, papa, what Dominie Vischer told us on Sunday, about blessings in disguise."

The image of the Dominie's reverend head, just visible above the huge high pulpit, and threatened with momentary demolition by the massive cone, which, like the sword of Damocles, hung perpetually above it, rose for a moment in Evert's mind.

"Yes—yes, my child, I remember it well," he replied. "Heaven knows I thought of thee when he spoke of the wind being tempered to the shorn lamb—for thou art a lamb, my Effie, and thy fold will soon be broken up."

We belong to one fold and one Shepherd, papa," said Effie, smiling cheerfully; and the old man, imprinting a kiss upon the cheek of his child, tottered weeping from the room.

# CHAPTER VII.

THE gallant Captain Sinclair, who bore about his person wounds received in the famous battle of Dunkirk, and who was loitering a while in this country, while awaiting some expected promotion on the navy rolls of Spain—the gallant Captain Sinclair was a little fond of play.

"Not deep—not deep, indeed," he would say, as, seating himself opposite the flattered Egbert in a small room of Mynheer Schnaffenswanzer's hotel, he would drop his cane and gloves, and, raising his eyeglass, gaze about the room with a quick, jerking motion of his head, to make sure that they were entirely alone. Captain Sinclair shuffled the cards very awkwardly. "We mariners," he would say, "are more accustomed to the boarding-pike than the card-table," and he quite envied his companion's more adroit and graceful motions. He was even known, at times, to drop a card on the floor, so very awkward was he, and so bungling, and at times those perverse little pieces of pasteboard would get even into the sleeves of the Captain's coat, a new naval undress of Spain, large at the wrist, and open, exceedingly.

He played often with Groesbeck, and sometimes, at night, in company also with a couple of young lieutenants in the Austrian service, with whom they had formed quite an accidental acquaintance, and the younger of whom took a great liking to Egbert, and was always his partner. They lost very heavily at times, but the Austrian bore his misfortunes with a good grace, and always paid promptly. So did Egbert, for he would not for the world have disgraced so distinguished an acquaintance.

And thus the poor dupe went on, floundering in the net that was all around him, and entangling himself at every throe more and more deeply. Not that Egbert and his companion always lost; on the contrary, they won at times quite considerable sums, which the Captain always paid down in broad Spanish pieces; but the preponderance of the luck was heavily against them, and, in the more private *tête-à-tête* games with the Spaniard, Egbert was also a heavy loser.

Sinclair consoled him, in all these reverses, with tales of the most astounding good fortune which had befallen people upon a sudden turn of luck after being nearly ruined.

Mr. Groesbeck did not seem much consoled by these anecdotes, for his losses continued to multiply, until their magnitude became truly alarming: but then the Captain was irresistibly polite and affable, and his victim could never find cause of quarrel or offence. Nor was their intimacy by any means confined to the card-table, for the Spaniard would often call with a dashing equipage purchased with his friend's money, and invite the latter to take a drive with him about the city and its suburbs. They were seen together, indeed, at all public places, and Egbert prided himself upon the association, for the Captain was so *distingué*.

There was one place, however, to which Sinclair never would go, however often invited or urged, and that was the residence of Mr. Hiram Sharp. He even seemed to avoid it in their drives about town, much to his companion's regret, for Egbert was not unwilling to show off his aristocratic-looking friend to Miss Euphemia, who, it need scarcely be said, was already fully reinstated in his affections. Scarcely a month had elapsed since the cessation of his visits to Effie, and it had been only out of fear of public scorn that he had even thus long refrained from appearing as the acknowledged suitor of Miss Sharp.

But such a motive was not likely long to influence him, more especially as neither the lawyer himself, nor his daughter, seemed to be troubled with any sensitiveness on that point. Sharp, indeed, for once became indiscreetly eager in the pursuit of his object, for the large bait, which, shark-like, he had so voraciously swallowed, seemed only to have whetted his appetite. The great Groesbeck estate being once in his family, in addition to his own now colossal fortune, he would be able to look down upon Governor Stuyvesant himself; while to have seen Egbert in the hands of the Knickerbockers, would have left his pique against that harmless old man far from being gratified.

It does not take long to make a bargain when both parties think they have got the best of it, and so the alliance was very soon agreed upon: the wedding-day was named, and the preparations went rapidly forward, and Sharp rode out to look at the estate and calculate its value in the hands of a good manager.

In the mean time Egbert continued his dangerous career, for the near approach of his wedding-day made him more anxious than ever to replenish his exchequer. He felt deeply the want of available funds, for although he had raised large sums by mortgaging his land, they had all passed into the hands of his adroit friend. He was resolved now to strike one Napoleonic blow for liberty, and, having fully recovered his ground, to be more wary in future about retaining it.

Elated with this resolution, which seemed so easy of accomplishment, he sought out Sinclair, and in the evening, in company with that gentleman, paid his accustomed visit to Mynheer Schnaffenswauzer's hotel. He felt certain that he should win on that night, and he resolved to risk larger sums than usual, in order that a short run of luck might set him up. He had before, on several occasions, blamed himself for the paltriness of his ventures, for, by an unfortunate coincidence, his winnings had almost always occurred when there was but little at stake.

"I have no more money," he said to Sinclair, laughing, as they again sat down at the fatal table; "Old Levi does nothing but croak, and make mouths, and twirl his long snaky fingers at me when I apply to him, and says he fears my estate is not worth what he has already advanced on it—the shrivelled old sinner. But I will put up the *acres* to-night, Captain Sinclair," he said, speaking with desperation. "You know that they are worth thrice the amount of the Jew's claim. What say you to the Harlem farm, where we shot that fine buck yesterday, against a thousand guineas?"

"What! play you so largely, then?" asked the other, with a surprised air.

The gleam of insanity was in the eye of Groesbeck, as he replied: "Ay—ay—it's this light play that ruins a man. Fortune smiles on a bold venture. Come, sir, down with your louis d'ors; I long to hear them chinking in my pockets."

The Spaniard's hesitation, whether real or affected, only increased the eagerness of his companion, and he at length complied. They played, and Egbert lost. His eye flashed wildly —his lips were compressed, but he did not complain. Another tract and another was proposed, and still Egbert lost, and thus half an hour elapsed, with but little variation of result. Three-fourths of Groesbeck's property was gone, and he was about pledging the remainder, when the Captain, alarmed lest by grasping at too much he might lose the whole, refused to play.

"The luck is clearly against you, to-night," he said; "do not tempt Fortune too far."

"I am ruined already," replied Egbert, dashing his cards to the floor; "three-fourths of my estate are in your hands; the rest will doubtless be the Jew's."

"Very true; very true," said Sinclair, blandly, and drawing on his gloves; "Count Sylvio——"

"D—n Count Sylvio!" said Egbert, tearing from his pocket a bundle of old papers, and flinging them upon the table. "There are my father's title-deeds; have your deeds prepared and send them to me at once, and they shall be executed; but do me the favor," he added, more mildly, "to keep this matter secret for one week."

"Most certainly, sir," said the Captain, clutching the papers, and feeling only half certain of his good fortune.

"One week, mind—and it will not matter so very much after all. Old *Hi*," he muttered to himself, thus abbreviating his expected father-in-law's name—"Old *Hi* is worth half a million."

And thus the gamblers parted.

## CHAPTER VIII.

It was on a calm May morning, about three days prior to that of the contemplated nuptials, that the virtuous Mr. Sharp was interrupted in the midst of a harangue at his own breakfast-table, upon the heavenliness of that charity which begins at home, by a visit from a friend of old standing, who desired to see him forthwith, alone, and on important business. Not a little surprised was the lawyer as, followed by the fierce-looking Captain Ripley, he led the way into a private apartment; for that enterprising mariner had now been in port so long that it was scarcely probable he could have any new bargains to offer. He was not, however, kept long in suspense. Mr. Ripley had called in behalf of a friend who was about to leave the country for a season, and who, having recently become an extensive land-holder in the province, was desirous of procuring a faithful agent to take charge of his estates.

Mr. Sharp was delighted; Mr. Sharp took off his spectacles and said: "Is it possible! yes—certainly—very discreet—happy to render him any service—always at the disposal of his friends," &c., &c.; and then Mr. Sharp put his spectacles on again, and waited meekly for further developments. They came. Captain Ripley was a man of very few words, and the story was soon told—as soon, that is, as the interruptions of the awfully incensed lawyer would permit. It is probably needless to say that Sinclair was the capitalist alluded to by Ripley, who, knowing nothing of the intended marriage between Egbert and Miss Sharp, and presuming upon the iniquitous bond of secrecy already existing between himself and Hiram, had not hesitated to hint broadly at the means by which his friend had acquired the Groesbeck estates.

"Mr. Ripley," said Hiram, as soon as his rage had subsided to the speaking point, "your friend is a swindler, and you are his accomplice, and the property must be refunded to Mr. Groesbeck at once, sir, or I will arrest you both, and for far graver crimes than this."

Sharp did not see—it would have been better for him if he had—the demoniac scowl and baleful glare which passed, like a cloud and a flash, across the sailor's face.

" You talk boldly, Mr. Sharp," he said, with composure.

" I do, sir," continued the lawyer; " I am a bold man; it is my business to be so. And mind, sir, I will have no parleying or delay in this matter; remember that there are trees on Gibbet Island that bear such fruit as you and your swindling companion."

" You are a bold man," replied Ripley; muttering a long foreign oath, which sounded like the rattling of shot against the inside of his teeth; " but what must be, must be. I will talk with Sinclair about it, and see what can be done."

" You had better—you had better," returned Sharp rapidly.

" I will see you——"

" This afternoon."

" I will;" and the sailor departed.

Manifest was Mr. Sharp's perturbation. He followed his visitor to the door, and followed him with his eyes far down the street, and waited anxiously for his return. He had known nothing before of Sinclair's connection with Ripley, and although he had long looked upon the former as some worthless adventurer, he had supposed him to be of a higher grade than the pirate; for such, he did not seek to conceal from his own mind, was Ralph. Before others he of course scouted the idea of such a suspicion, for his own business connection with the sailor and his companions had of late been scarcely cloaked. His present dilemma was therefore a serious one; for even if he had possessed sufficient evidence for the arrest of Ralph and his friend on so grave a charge as piracy, he would, by so doing, impugn his own moral character, a fabric which stood already on too tottering a basis to bear any very heavy concussion. He would also put a stop to a very lucrative business, derived not alone from the harmless little Zephyr, Captain Ripley, of and for Lisbon, and now lying at anchor on the opposite side of the bay, just out of reach of the guns of the fort; but from several other similar craft floating under the colors of Portugal and Spain, and visiting at times the harbor of Manhattan.

Besides all this there was, in reality, no sufficient legal proof against either Ralph or his vessel, and he knew very well that Lovelace would never consent to embroil himself, uselessly, with a set of desperadoes, who, in one way or another, would be sure to have their revenge. He had heard, however, that outlaws of this description were proverbially timid, beneath all their outside swagger, and his hope lay chiefly in the fears which he had evidently excited in Ripley's breast.

Several hours elapsed, and the day was on the decline, when Ralph returned. A tall stout man he was, brown as a butternut, and sporting bushy black whiskers, and a mustache. The lawyer's mind was wonderfully relieved on seeing him, for there was such a good-natured, playful smile upon his face, and his glittering teeth shone out so frankly from between their black borders, that he felt satisfied all was right. They conversed awhile apart, but the store was thronged with people, and there was so little room for privacy, that Hiram, at the suggestion of his visitor, took his hat, and they sauntered slowly down the street. The Captain talked rapidly and seemingly to the point, for his auditor was very attentive. He grew eloquent, indeed, and his arms flew about like flails, and his head went bobbing in every direction.

"My friend, Captain Sinclair," he said, "is a gentleman of the strictest honor, I do assure you, sir; and he charges me to say to you, that if he could only once have dreamed of such a thing —if he could just have *dreamed* of it, sir, that your daughter was to be married to Mr. Groesbeck, he certainly would not—would not—have—have——"

"Fleeced him!" suggested Hiram!

"No, no, no! my *dear* sir, that's not the word; you are facetious, you are, indeed, sir."

To this and a great deal more, Sharp listened anxiously, expecting momentarily to hear something to the point. They had left the main thoroughfare to avoid listeners, and were strolling through a by-street, towards the river, at a point but little frequented, and near to which the water was fringed with a thin growth of bushes. Hiram had been all eagerness and delight; for he was too cunning to be taken in by any professions of regard on the part of Ralph and Sinclair, and attributed all his companion's civility to the fright which his threats had occasioned him. Indeed, he had been so accustomed of late to see people cringe to him, that he had begun to fancy himself a man of extraordinary importance. But some how or other there did not seem to be quite that degree of fear manifested by his companion which he had expected, and he recalled all his former sternness of manner that he might re-awaken it, and bring matters to a more speedy conclusion.

"Well, well, Mr. Ripley, this is all well enough," he said. "but where are the deeds? These, you know, must be returned at once."

"The deeds—ah, yes. Captain Sinclair says—this way a little, the walking is better," taking a side-cut across an unfenced field, and still towards the river and the bushes—"Captain Sinclair says that he will surrender them with the greatest pleasure in the world——"

Hiram's eyes sparkled——

"Upon your paying him ten thousand guineas!"

"The scoundrel!" exclaimed Sharp, blinded again by sudden rage; "does he dare, do *you* dare to make such a proposal? Do you remember what I said to you this morning?"

"I DO," returned Ripley, through his teeth, and letting his brawny hand fall with the clutch of a tiger upon the shoulder of his companion; "I remember it *well*," he said, dragging the other within the cover of the bushes, "*you said there were trees on Gibbet Island which bore such fruit as I and my swindling companion.*"

The pirate's face was changed to that of a demon; his eyes were bloodshot his nostrils were dilated; his cheeks were flushed; and his whole frame quivered with the intensity of his rage.

"You, Hiram Sharp, who have fattened on my favors—whose whole life has been full of fraud and villainy—who yourself deserve the death of a dog—do you talk to *me* about the *gibbet!*"

"My good sir, I didn't mean——"

"Nay, it is *too late!*" thundered Ralph, shaking his victim to make him stand still.

"Really, really, my dear Captain Ripley, let us go back,—never mind the deeds; never mind the property."

"*It is too late!*"

"I will pay the ten thousand——"

"*It is too late!*"

A long, low whistle issued from the lips of Ralph, and two agile seamen sprang up the bank and stood at his side. Bound, gagged, dragged down the declivity, and thrust into a small boat which lay concealed beneath the bushes, Sharp's failing senses became conscious only of a rapid transition across the water, of being hoisted up the side of a ship, and thrown, like a log, into some dark corner.

Ralph had remained on the beach, and strolling leisurely back to the city, he took especial pains to exhibit himself at all his accustomed places of resort. He even called at Sharp's shop, and, not finding its proprietor at home, patiently awaited his return, smoking meanwhile a fantastically carved pipe, and imbibing a liberal potation of his friend's double-reduced Monongahela.

Hiram in the mean time remained in the dreadful situation which has been described, a prey to the most excruciating terror. All his efforts to move or speak were unavailing, and the only sound that reached his ears was an occasional coarse jibe upon his misfortunes, followed by fiendish laughter. Hours elapsed, he knew not how many. The day went and came, and there he lay. But at length there was the sound of an approaching boat, and cheerful voices were heard without. Somebody had come; there was a faint gleam of hope in his breast. His son

3

had proved vigilant and shrewd; had suspected his fate; had incited the governor to action; had arrested the kidnappers, and flown, armed with official authority, to his relief. Such was the dream of a moment, and in the next Ralph and Sinclair stood before him—*smiling!* Oh, how dreadful was that smile! His whole frame shuddered as he saw it, for it spoke of the poniard, the gurgling waters, and the shark! He was brought forward, and the gag was removed from his mouth, but he could not speak. His feet were next pinioned together, yet only by gestures could he express his agony.

"Bring a small shot forward!" shouted Ralph.

"Ay, ay, sir," was the quick response, and a twelve-pound ball was brought.

"Fasten it to his feet," he said, turning away, "and, when it is quite dark, call me."

Again the answer was prompt, and the orders were obeyed, and Ralph and Sinclair descended to the cabin. Hiram's senses seemed spell-bound, as it were, by some hideous nightmare; but he recovered his voice at length, and called faintly to one of his guards. He came nearer.

"Do you want to be rich?" whispered the prisoner, "very rich?—do you want gold—gold—ten thousand real glittering guineas?"

"Yes," said the sailor.

"Help me to escape, and you shall have it all—all—and more."

"*There are trees on Gibbet Island that bear such fruit as we!*" was the taunting reply.

It was as if some mocking demon was ever echoing back the words of his rash threat. He was about to renew his efforts when Ralph and Sinclair approached. The evening had set in, and it was already sufficiently dark to prevent any possibility of observation from the shore. At their approach Hiram poured forth the most frantic cries for pity, and Sinclair seemed suddenly to relent.

"Stop, Ralph," he said, as they were dragging their victim to the side of the ship. "We sail in a few weeks—let's carry the old sinner to the Pelews."

"Yes, gentlemen, yes," cried Sharp; "do—do—I'll Christianize them."

"I'll not consent to it," exclaimed Ripley, with an oath—"he would have hung us; let him die—I won't consent to it."

"Your consent won't be asked, Mr. Ripley," returned the other coolly. "You forget yourself, I think—perhaps you have been a little too long on shore."

" Very true, Captain—it's for you to say, of course, but it's my game, and curse me if I think it's hardly fair."

"Oh, never mind, Ralph ; I'll promise you he never sets foot on these shores again, and that's enough for our purposes."

Poor Hiram had remained looking from one to the other of his captors during this colloquy in a tumult of dreadful emotions ; but when he felt himself relieved from the prospect of immediate death his delight was unbounded. The shot was removed, and he was secured, still bound, in a small room below.

## CHAPTER IX

RUDOLPH GROESBECK did not cherish his grief, or seek to perpetuate an illusory hope. But let him not be blamed if he could not at once uproot the gentle flower of affection, which, dear to him as the stricken gourd to the rebellious prophet of Judah, had sprung into existence with almost equal celerity. Isolated from the ordinary ties of life, it was natural that his one attachment should be intense and strong. He struggled indeed to free himself from its power, but, like the broken slumbers of morning, it still returned to enthral him, and like disturbed dreams its gorgeous fragments still re-united, and glowed as brilliantly as ever. The winter had passed slowly away, and the mellow skies of May were bending above Fort Orange, and the quiet little hamlet which surrounded it.

It was high noon in Albany, the hour of sleep from time immemorial to the Netherlanders, and in peaceful oblivion were its ancient burghers wrapt. There was fortunately an English garrison at the fort, or the wily Hurons would have found it as safe an hour for attack as the noon of night; and it is even reported on as good authority as that of Herr Longbow Vondermarvel, a now neglected chronicler, that in earlier days the Dutch sentinels had been scalped while asleep upon the walls, and had only discovered their loss on awaking at the usual hour. The regretted trophies, however, it is said, had been subsequently returned to them by the taunting foe, well cured and smoked, and suitable for use as tobacco-pouches.

But there was a sudden commotion in the sleep-enveloped village, on the day which has just been described. Doors and window-shutters were thrown violently open in every direction, and heads were peering out and clamorous voices were heard; and one little bandy-legged fellow, with a short pipe fitted immovably in one corner of his mouth, was flying about from house to house, sputtering forth something in deep Dutch which elicited a general jabbering response from all quarters, whether of joy or grief, it was difficult to tell. The men shouted, the women yelled, the hens cackled, and the dogs frisked about, and snuffed the air, and barked, and wondered what the deuce was in the wind.

"Who saw it, Hans Spaffenswelter?" asked old David Groesbeck, who had come growling from his sleep,—"that's what I want to know—who saw it?"

"Josh Vanderwater saw it," was the triumphant reply; "Josh Vanderwater, and you'll allow he's got eyes."

An apparent commotion at the fort was also perceptible, for the commandant and half the garrison were on the walls, shading their eyes with their hands, and peering away down the river. There was a sloop coming up the Hudson, that is to say, she was lying becalmed about ten miles distant, and might safely be expected in within forty-eight hours. She had come all the way from New York, and had escaped all the dangers of that long and perilous route. She would bring news from the city, news of distant friends, news, perhaps, even from Faderland, that distant world, to which the memory of many an ancient Hollander still clung with a fervent love, not to be superseded or effaced.

Well might they rejoice! Well might the old cronies congregate together on the sunny beach, and shake hands, and laugh, and anticipate the tidings! How did *they* know but the lower fort and city were again in the hands of the Dutch? for many were still firm in the belief of such a restoration. Ah, how would their old hearts have bounded at such tidings! How they would have rushed with a shout to the feebly garrisoned fort—pulled down its hated flag, and raised the banners of the mighty States of Holland to the northern breeze! Well might they rejoice, for they were a noble-hearted, simple-minded race, full of honest patriotism, and lofty courage, and patient endurance.

Rudolph alone heard of the approach of the vessel without joy. To him it could only bring tidings of grief. He would hear of the consummation of his misery; he would hear that an eternal barrier was placed between himself and the one object of his affections. Such were his thoughts, and when, on the next day, a favoring breeze brought the sloop into port, and the city rushed *en masse* to the wharf, he strolled nervously away to the forests, that he might postpone for a little while the certainty of his woe. He was not missed from that excited throng, where friends abroad were shouting to friends on shore; where old men tottered on their canes, and leaned earnestly forward, and placed their hands behind their ears to catch the shouted tidings; where each eagerly asked what it was, and none could tell, and hope, and fear, and expectation reigned, and Babel's uproar was all renewed. Clustered like bees upon the pier, mounted on boxes and barrels, clinging to posts and corners, and all as eager and delighted as children at a show, thus the people watched and waited for the slow-moving sloop.

"Hef you got any latters?" shouted old Myndert Van Schaick, from the top of a populous hogshead, and waving his cane to attract attention; and the reply was in pantomime, by the captain taking from his capacious waistcoat pocket a large package, and holding it up to view, thereby visibly increasing the excitement on shore.

"Is the ship in?" "Is there any news from Holland?" "What tidings from the war?" "What news of Admiral De Ruyter?" "How's old Governor Stuyvesant?" Such were the questions resounding on all sides.

"There is a ship just in," was the reply sung out by stentorian lungs from the vessel; "news of a great—naval—battle; Admiral De Ruyter vic-*tor-r-r*-ious!" and then the welkin rang with huzzas, and tears gushed forth, and congratulations were exchanged on all sides. For this, it will be remembered, was the period when Charles the Second and Louis the Fourteenth had coolly resolved to slice up the Lowlands, and, allowing the Prince of Orange a moiety for his connivance, to divide the residue between themselves—a very fair business transaction, to which the Dutch were unreasonable enough to object, and flying to their arms, or rather to their fleets, under the invincible De Ruyter, fought three drawn battles with the allied navies of France and England, and taught them not to look for honey in hornets' nests. It was a tyrant's war, waged in opposition to the sympathies of the British people, who, with unexampled magnanimity, wept at the reverses of their foes, and rejoiced at their own defeats.

It was not until the tumult had subsided, and the crowd had dispersed, that Rudolph, still futilely trying to throw aside his dejection, proceeded slowly homeward. He was met by his good-natured uncle, with an open letter in his hand, the reading of which he had not yet completed. He proceeded rapidly to relate to Rudolph the only prominent item of news of which he had as yet become possessed, which was the extraordinary misfortune of Evert Knickerbocker. Startling as was this intelligence, which was discussed at length, and with deep regret, it conveyed no gleam of hope to Rudolph's mind, for he had no doubt that the nuptials of Egbert and Effie were already solemnized, and he now waited patiently until he should hear it announced.

The old man put on his spectacles, and, holding the letter up to the light, resumed its perusal. Various desultory items of intelligence next followed, and Rudolph listened long with exemplary patience, but he was about turning away when his attention was arrested by the mention of his brother's name.

"Egbert Groesbeck," continued the old man, still reading aloud, "is—to be—married—"

Rudolph's heart stood still—

" In—about—three—weeks—to—to "—a pause of considerable length ensued—

" *Effie*, uncle, *Effie Knickerbocker*," exclaimed Rudolph at length with desperation, and anxious to have it done with.

" To—to—," said the old man, holding the letter still closer, and peering earnestly at the puzzling characters ; " to—to—"

" EFFIE, I tell you," said Rudolph, who, unable longer to endure the torture, seized his hat and was hastening from the room, when his uncle began to spell the refractory word.

" E-u-p-h, Eff——"

Three chairs lay rolling about the floor, which had obstructed Rudolph's leap to his uncle's side ; he snatched the letter from the astonished old man, and holding it with a hand that shook till the paper rattled with the motion, he read the name, " *Euphemia Sharp!*"

" The scoundrel!" exclaimed old Groesbeck, heedless of his nephew's emotion.

Flushed with excitement, Rudolph tarried long enough only to read a few succeeding paragraphs in the letter, confirmatory of the news, and then hastened to seek some retirement where he might give way to his emotions. Hope had burst upon his mind with a radiance almost too dazzling for endurance. Effie was free, and was no longer separated from him by the formidable barrier of wealth. *She was free to be wooed and won by him.* How his rapt heart exulted at the thought, which, for a while, buoyed him up above all doubts and apprehensions. True, he was poor, but poverty is a remediable evil. The gates of wealth and power must ever yield to the magical *sesame* of an iron resolution ; and what would he not dare and do, inspirited by such a hope ? The world, from that moment, assumed a new aspect to his view. Life was no longer a load to be endured, but a gift to be prized and cherished. The earth was changed from a vast prison-house to a blooming Paradise, teeming with beauty and redolent of fragrance.

O blessed Hope! if thy sister, Faith, can remove mountains in the natural world, thou canst remove them from the human heart. It was with no light regret that Rudolph's friends heard him announce his determination to return to New York in the vessel which had just arrived, and which was to descend the river within a few weeks. But entreaties were unavailing to prolong his stay. Let us behold him then again voyaging the mighty Hudson, and, after a speedy trip of twelve days, once more arrived at the metropolis.

# CHAPTER X.

THE time of Rudolph's return was about ten days prior to the period appointed for the nuptials of Egbert and Miss Sharp, and of course about a week before the abduction of the lawyer. The intended wedding, however, was far from being a matter of public notoriety, and was entirely unknown to Mr. Knickerbocker, who continued to cherish the hope that Egbert's estrangement was only temporary, and that he would yet prove mindful of his obligations. He knew but little indeed of the true character of the individual whom he thus desired as the protector of his daughter, and still less of Effie's feelings in regard to him.

Long accustomed to wealth, and to the influence which it commands, he had insensibly acquired the habit of considering it essential to happiness, and nothing gave him more uneasiness than the dread of leaving his child unprotected by so powerful an ægis. Although Egbert's vices were radical, and indicated almost a total absence of moral principle, his manner, as has been said, was frank and engaging. Smiles were ever at his command—counterfeits, of course, of the heart's true currency, but which, like other counterfeits, were freely dispensed. It was not strange, therefore, that the guileless Evert, who was possessed of that blessed spirit of Charity which "thinketh no evil," still retained confidence in the son of his deceased friend.

There was one exception to the universality of Egbert's smiles. He had none for Rudolph; and, so far from welcoming him home, gave manifest tokens of dissatisfaction at his return. The intercourse of the brothers was of course, therefore, of the most limited kind, for however Rudolph's generous nature would have induced him to cultivate a more fraternal feeling, his advances were ever coldly repulsed, and were even openly attributed to motives of personal interest.

Rudolph was fortunately charged with some friendly mes-

sages from his uncle to Mr. Knickerbocker, and, as may be
imagined, he was not tardy in calling to deliver them. As he
approached Evert's residence, he saw the old man from a distance, now strolling slowly through his garden, and now leaning on his cane at the water-side, and looking wistfully in the
direction of his lost estates. As he came nearer, he saw Effie
also, restraining her buoyant steps, and walking slowly at her
dear father's side; and a still nearer view would have shown
him that her face was radiant with smiles, and that her lips
were prattling of hope, and that she was full of little devices to
win the heart-broken Evert from his grief; for she trembled,
poor Effie, for the failing reason of her sire, as, with his thin
locks streaming to the wind, he still gazed silently away—far
away—toward the miles of blooming fields and waving forests
which were even yet called by his name.

Although nearly a stranger to the family, Rudolph received
a cordial welcome from the hospitable old man, who congratu-
lated him on his safe return, and evinced much curiosity on the
subject of his adventures. Effie, delighted at the returning
smiles of her father, and at the interest which he manifested in
their visitor's narrative, became a deeply interested listener,
and was doubly beautiful, because utterly unconscious of being
the object of admiration. Rudolph, of course, exerted himself
to please, and became astonished at his own resources, and
when he rose to take his leave his new friends parted with him
with unfeigned regret.

It was a singular accident, Effie thought, that on the very
next day she met him again, while taking a short walk, and
that he strolled at her side, and engaged her in conversation,
and accompanied her home, and again sat down by old Evert's
side for two long hours. On the ensuing day he came to exhibit some northern curiosity of which he had spoken on a
former visit, and on the next, for some other easily invented
cause. How very kind it was of him, thought sweet unsuspecting Effie, to come thus daily and cheer up poor papa, for
the old man's eyes always brightened at his approach, and all
his grief seemed for a while forgotten.

But other eyes soon brightened, and other ears caught first
the sound of his footsteps, and an angel heart beat quicker at
his coming. New and strange emotions were Effie's, uncon-
fessed to herself, and carefully concealed from others. Vainly
she sought to repress them, or to believe that they did not
exist; for she did not dare to believe that Rudolph's visits
were intended for her, or that he looked upon her with any
especial regard. To her appreciating heart he was all too
noble and too pure, to be within the attractions of her humble

3*

charms. But as day after day brought some new token of his regard, the delighted Effie was compelled to believe and hope, and to look tremblingly for that avowal, which seemed only unspoken.

But Rudolph unfortunately began to be haunted by doubts. The first ardor of his hopes had subsided, and some very natural fears suggested themselves to his mind. If Effie had really been attached to Egbert, was it not reasonable to suppose that she still loved him? Might she not even be cherishing the expectation of his returning fealty; and might not her present kindness to himself be the more freely exhibited, because she had every reason to believe that he knew of her love for another, and that he would not misconstrue her friendship into affection? Lovers are always skilled in self-torture, and Rudolph was fast becoming a proficient in the art. Several unfortunate circumstances gave strength to his suspicions, and, just as he had resolved to hear the worst from Effie herself, a most untoward event occurred, interrupting his design, and dashing all his brilliant hopes to earth.

Evert had continued blind to the attachment which existed between Effie and Rudolph, and so pertinaciously had his own thoughts and hopes clung to the idea of Egbert's returning faith, that he imagined his daughter to be imbued with the same feelings. What else, he thought, could render her so happy and contented? How could her step be otherwise so light, her voice so cheerful, her face so radiant with smiles? In this state of mind the half-crazed father applied to poor Rudolph for his opinion in regard to the extent of Egbert's defection, and the probability of his return; and when the young man found voice to reply, it was only hurriedly to inquire if Effie would still be a willing party to the alliance with his brother.

The surprised air of Evert, as he returned an unhesitating answer in the affirmative, set the seal to Rudolph's despair. He felt like one who, having in a dream climbed to some giddy eminence, topples suddenly from its summit. He was now furnished, he thought, with the key to all Effie's conduct. His sagacity had been at fault before, only because it had been led blindfold by his hopes. But he never would hope again. Rudolph, in short, discontinued his visits to Effie, and betook himself once more to solitude, but, as is supposed, not of the "sweetened" variety.

# CHAPTER XI.

The mysterious disappearance of Mr. Sharp caused an unexampled commotion in the community. Wells were explored, and rivers dragged, and forests searched in a fruitless effort to bring his mortal remains to light, and among the crowds who engaged in these labors, none were more active or efficient than Ralph Ripley. The excitement was continually increased by some new rumor on the subject, and conjectures of every description were of course afloat. Some said that the trading Indians had carried him off, in payment of certain arrearages of indebtedness, and there were not wanting others, who, exonerating the savages, still shook their heads gravely, and said it was what they had long expected. A certain personage *would* have his own, and probably Sharp had got no more than he had bargained for a great while before.

No suspicion fell on Ripley, for none had known of the quarrel on the day of the abduction, and until that time Ralph and the lawyer had been on friendly terms. As to Sinclair, he gave himself no uneasiness on the subject, excepting to express an opinion that it was really quite a shocking affair; but he had known many things more strange off the coast of Portugal. But when three or four days had elapsed without any clew to the secret, the search was relinquished, and poor Sharp was abandoned to his fate. The wedding was of course postponed, and Egbert Groesbeck had the gratifying prospect before him, not only of utter insolvency, but of a speedy exposure of his affairs, and probably a perpetual leave of absence from the charming Euphemia. Neither that young lady, nor her brother, manifested any excess of grief at their misfortune, for Sharp had been in his family, as elsewhere, a harsh man, and his house had been emphatically a home of the iron rule.

Benhadad was a young man of a lofty gait, and a general pompousness of mien. His self-importance, never deficient, had been immeasurably increased by his new position, and it was with difficulty that he could keep down his sense of rising greatness sufficiently to admit of paying decent respect to the memory of his lost parent. He possessed, of course, but little of his father's shrewdness, for arrogance in his case, as in most others, was the offspring of a shallow brain ; but then he fully believed that the cloak of Hiram had fallen upon his shoulders, and that it was an exceeding good fit.

But Hiram Sharp, in the mean time, as the reader is aware, had not yet put off his mortal coil. His prison chamber was lighted by a port-hole, the iron tenant of which was stored for the present, with its companions, beneath a miscellaneous mass of ballast, far from the observation of any prying eyes, which might, upon some possible contingency, visit the suspected Zephyr. The port-holes themselves were ingeniously masked, this one alone being left partly unclosed, less, however, out of any regard for the prisoner's comfort, than for the convenience of his custodians. Sharp was chained to the floor, at a point whence it was supposed impossible for him to gain access to the aperture, even to indulge in the slight luxury of gazing upon the world from which he was excluded.

But what will not the ingenuity of despair, favored by solitude, accomplish? By dint of extraordinary muscular exertions, and untiring patience, he could succeed in bringing his eyes to a level with the opening, and feasting them upon the view without, taking care, of course, never to indulge in this forbidden pleasure when there was any danger of being discovered by his keepers. The window looked out upon the distant city. He could see his own house, and watch the very smoke that curled up from the fireside at which he had been accustomed to sit. He could see figures moving at the open windows, and others crossing the lawn, and entering his doors ; and, when the air was still and dense, he could even hear the barking of his favorite dog. The voice and its echo from the barn came to him together.

Day and night did Hiram gaze, at intervals, through this "loop-hole of his retreat" toward his distant home. It seemed as if it had been prepared for him by way of a refined species of torture ; for not Tantalus, bound chin-deep in the cool waters which his parched lips might never reach, not Tantalus endured a more exquisite pain. But there is only one place to which Hope never comes, and that good genius appeared to Hiram in the very remarkable guise of old Tony West, a negro fisherman. Tony was the property of a main-chance man on Long Island, who, in consideration of his faithful services by day, generously allowed him his liberty at night, a portion of which the slave regularly appropriated to his piscatory pursuits, and was thereby amassing, by sixpences, a sum with which to purchase, at some future day, no less a treasure than his own body and soul.

"Some men are born free," thought Tony, sadly, "and that's five hundred dollars in their pockets to start with;" but still he did not complain, but went on toiling with net and line, fully believing that he should yet fish up the great boon of liberty from the bottom of the bay. He had reason to hope, Tony had; for a year's labor had brought him nearly fifty dollars; a stupendous sum in his imagination, and only nine years more would complete the task.

It was on a dark night that the negro, after unusually long and ineffectual labors in his little skiff, far out from shore, had raised his anchor dejectedly and started for home. The night was far spent, and his torches had expired, and his pipe had gone out, and he bent, nodding with sleep, over his oars, yet keeping up their slow and monotonous stroke, and lulling himself still more by the sound. But, as Morpheus gained ground, the oars dropped from his hands, and the dark boat, and its darker tenant, drifted silently along, invisible as a cloud upon the wave.

If Tony did not catch many fish in his sleep, it was not for want of diligent bobbing, for his round woolly head went up and down with a ceaseless and regular motion, and he was only awakened at length from a dreamy tussle with a mammoth fish, by the sound of his boat striking against some hard substance. It was some time before he became sufficiently awake to discover that he had run foul of a ship, and he was about pushing his boat off, when he heard a voice calling in an earnest but suppressed tone for help. The negro could see nothing, but he guided his skiff in the direction of the sound, and soon lay directly beneath the point whence it seemed to emanate.

"Quick—quick," said the prisoner—"this way—listen to me; I am Hiram Sharp, the great merchant of New York— kidnapped by Captain Ripley—and going to be murdered here on board the Zephyr—do you hear me?"

"Y—y—yes," said Tony, trembling, "I hare."

"Who are you?" said Sharp.

"Tony—Tony—I'm Tony—I b'long to Massa West, over yeer in Breuklyn."

"Go quick to my son and tell him where I am—murdered— on the Zephyr—quick—and tell him to give you a hundred dollars, right straight down—and that I say so. Go, Tony— good Tony, quick."

"Jess jump right out, massa—right out of that hole."

"Oh, I can't, Tony, I can't; my feet are chained together, and chained to the floor; go, Tony, go."

.And Tony went.

The ensuing morning had been set apart by Mr. Benhadad Sharp for a visit to the manor tenantry, to notify them of their loss, and that he, Benhadad, was to be regarded as their future landlord. His buttoned coat only did not burst, as, clad in the habiliments of woe, he stepped into his carriage, and was detained only by the sudden appearance of Tony, breathless and speechless, who, gazing at him with eyes frightfully dilated, laid his huge dark hand upon the wheel, as if he would arrest its motion until he could speak. Benhadad waited complacently, for he knew the old negro well, and had no doubt that he had brought intelligence of having accidentally fished up his honored ancestor. Indeed, he was already singling out a small coin in his pocket to reward the slave, when the latter recovered his voice, and with chattering teeth related his wonderful tale.

Astonishment and alarm for a moment held the young man silent. Tumultuous and mingled feelings succeeded, in which, strange to tell, joy did not preponderate. His dimensions visibly diminished, and his swollen and rigid air quite disappeared. He questioned the negro again and again, and, eliciting nothing to throw discredit on the story, dismissed him. To Tony's eager appeal for the promised reward, he replied by a gratuity of half a dollar, and an intimation that a similar sum would be forthcoming after the release of his father was effected. No injunction of secrecy was imposed upon the negro; nothing to prevent the rumor from spreading, reaching the ears of Ripley, and thus defeating the chance of rescue.

But Tony was not himself devoid of sagacity, and his wits were sharpened now by the hope of gaining the munificent prize which had been promised him. He hastened therefore, unobserved by Benhadad, to the presence of Euphemia, and, repeating his marvellous tale, again demanded his reward. Miss Sharp was both shocked and delighted, for she was not without a degree of affection for her father, and besides that, she was not unmindful of her deferred nuptials. Egbert was at once summoned, and he indeed proved a joyful recipient of the news, and advised instant, vigorous, and secret action; while Benhadad, who soon joined them, found himself compelled to imitate the zeal of his companions, and was even forced by their decision to tell down the chinking gold into poor Tony's broad, black, trembling hand.

How it glistened on that ebony palm! How melodiously they rung, those twenty bright yellow guineas, striking against each other, and how the great iron fingers closed over the treasure, with a clutch designed to render all relentings useless. Nothing but Death could have opened Tony's hand.

Egbert went about his task with earnestness. Enjoining the

strictest secrecy upon all, his first step was to lay all the facts before Governor Lovelace, and apply for his official aid. He had a long and private interview with that officer, and was returning from the government house, wrapt in the contemplation of his schemes, when he encountered Captain Sinclair, bearing in his hands a package of papers, which he at once recognized as the fatal deeds. They were in the vicinity of the office of records, and Egbert at once guessed the design of the other; for he had been daily trembling at the expected exposure of his affairs, and had with difficulty persuaded his friend to defer making the matter public until now. Taking the arm of Sinclair, and drawing him aside, he said—"You have accommodated me so often about these dreadful deeds, that I really feel ashamed to ask any further delay; but let me beg for one week more."

"Mr. Groesbeck must excuse me," answered Sinclair, coldly; "the deeds must be recorded."

"Give me one week," said Egbert, "and you will save me from ruin."

Sinclair smiled incredulously, and did not yield; it was the old story, he said, and Groesbeck was no nearer his object now than he had been three weeks before.

"Stop," said Egbert, as the other was turning away; "I have a great secret; you shall hear it, and judge for yourself."

He then proceeded to relate to the astonished Sinclair the discoveries in relation to Sharp, and how his return would be followed in a few days by the postponed wedding. "A warrant is already being prepared for Ripley's arrest," he said, "and as soon as it is dark, three gunboats with marines will be sent out to board the Zephyr, and bring her into port. Do you believe me now," he said, "and will you wait?"

"I do—I do," replied Sinclair, smiling, and returning the papers to his pocket. "Oh yes—I'll wait; why, there'll be fun, won't there? I wonder if they'll hang that bull-dog of a Ripley. I always thought he had a bad look—the scoundrel—the dem'd infernal villain, I may say. Good morning—good morning, sir;" and bowing and smiling, Captain Sinclair turned gracefully away, leaving Egbert more than ever impressed with the idea that he was an exceedingly civil and good-natured fellow.

Twenty minutes afterwards Sinclair and Ralph were standing together in the very grove which had proved so fatal to Hiram.

"You will cruise in the West Indies until autumn," said Sinclair, hurriedly, "when you will return to Boston, where I will meet you. In the mean time, you will of course change your paint and name."

"And that d—d Sharp?" said Ripley, inquiringly, as he placed one foot in the boat, and looked angrily back.

"Is TO BE PRESERVED," said Sinclair emphatically; "mind, I insist on this; the reason you shall know hereafter."

"I'll be hanged if he don't wish the sharks had him, then, before we get back," replied Ripley, as he pushed off; and Sinclair, smiling, walked hurriedly back to offer his assistance in the pursuit.

## CHAPTER XII.

FORMIDABLE, meanwhile, were the preparations which were made for the seizure of the Zephyr. The suspicion which had long rested upon this vessel was now turned into a reasonable certainty, and Governor Lovelace, roused to vigorous action by so great an outrage, was determined to bring her into port, and to arrest her whole crew as pirates, not doubting that the fullest proof could be adduced against them. There was no naval force in any shape attached to the colonial government at this period; but there was fortunately a British man-of-war lying in port, undergoing some repairs, which, although unfitted for immediate service, was manned by a gallant crew and brave officers, of whom Mr. Second Lieutenant Flash was one.

To his charge the expedition was committed, which was to be, if necessary, a regular "cutting out" affair, although it was hoped that the enemy, being unalarmed, would offer no serious resistance. Not so, however, hoped Flash, who, from the moment that he was intrusted with the enterprise, considered his long-expected promotion as secured beyond any further contingency.

All day did Egbert Groesbeck walk excitedly about, watching the mysterious preparations; for no one felt more anxious than he about the result. He feared momentarily that the Zephyr would take to flight, for she seemed like some graceful sea-bird, floating buoyantly upon the water, and ready to spread her white wings at the least alarm. There seemed, however, little ground for such an apprehension, for she had lain for weeks in her present position, and gave no indication of any intended change. The failure to find Ripley on shore created no surprise, for he frequently passed days together on his ship, and he was supposed to be in profound ignorance of the deep and well-digested designs against him.

Motionless meanwhile, and with no appearance of life upon her decks, lay the suspected Zephyr. The wind was light, and was growing gradually less, and Ripley avoided exhibiting any premonitions of flight, until the breeze was sufficient to render the attempt effectual; for if he was to be compelled to await an attack, it was better that the enemy should suppose him to be unalarmed. He relied, however, on the wind freshening at sunset, enough at least to admit of changing his position to some good hiding-place, and in the night or the early morning, the zephyrs would be pretty certain to come to the assistance of their graceful little namesake. "Two or three puffs," he said, looking aloft with knotted brows, "will put her outside the Narrows, and then we are safe." Ripley would have fought the boats with a perfect good will, had not Sinclair forbidden it, and then besides, he thought, this fighting with a halter around one's neck isn't exactly the thing. His guns were mounted, however, and all his weapons were put in order to repel an attack, and it was not a little singular that two diligent subordinate officers who superintended these labors bore a marvellous resemblance to the Austrian lieutenants, of whom mention has heretofore been made.

All day did Ralph watch the sky and scan the light feathery clouds to find tokens of the coming wind—but all in vain: the breeze continued to fall away, and when the sun went down there was a perfect calm. So smooth and motionless lay the waters that the stars, as they successively came to their posts, were greeted by their images in the wide and beautiful mirror which lay stretched beneath them. The situation of the Zephyr became momentarily more critical, and Ripley began to give tokens of uneasiness. Even the tide had joined the list of his enemies. It was coming slowly in, and any attempt to change his position, by drifting, would have borne him still further from the open sea, and would thus have diminished his chances of escape.

Meanwhile Lieutenant Flash was the busiest and happiest man in the province. It was about nine o'clock that he put his force in motion, after a brief hortatory address to his men, reminding them that the honor of their flag, their own private reputation, and a small fortune for each of them, depended upon their conduct.

"It's probable," he said, "mind I don't say it's certain, but it's probable that fellow is ballasted with ingots. Remember that the most perfect silence is to be maintained, and you all understand that, one way or another, we are to bring the Zephyr into port;" and touching his cap to Governor Lovelace and Captain Grim, who, with one or two others, stood wrapt in their cloaks on the quarter-deck of "the Terror," watching the embarkation, the gallant lieutenant sat down, and the boats, with muffled oars, moved noiselessly off. It is needless to say that every man resolved to be first on board the enemy, and, with such enthusiasm, there was little fear of defeat.

As the twilight had departed, Ripley's alarm had rapidly increased. The unfurled sails were hanging motionless from the masts, ready for the wind, which did not come; and one, with an axe, stood ready to cut the huge cable at the first rustling of the air. But still the seemingly doomed vessel lay,

> "—— without breath or motion,
>  As idle as a painted ship
>  Upon a painted ocean."

Every preparation was therefore made for the conflict which now seemed unavoidable; and although the Zephyr was but slightly manned, the fierce looks and threats of the bold buccaneers showed that she would prove no easy prey. The disadvantage of the pirates consisted in being greatly outnumbered, and in the fact that their enemy, if beaten off, could reinforce his strength, and renew the attack. As to the guns of the ship, but little aid was expected from them in the silence and obscurity of a night attack, when the first notice of their foe might be the clash of the grappling irons. An hour elapsed, and a distinct though faint sound of oars was heard. Every heart beat quicker.

"Zephyr, ahoy, ahoy!" came up in a faint but familiar voice from under the bow.

"It's _the Captain!_" responded twenty voices in a breath, and, before the buzz of excitement had subsided, Sinclair stood upon the deck.

"I knew Captain Karl wasn't the man to see his comrades fighting against odds, and he not there," said a privileged old ruffian, with an oath.

"No, no, my boys," replied the Captain, evidently in a state of the most intense excitement; "no, no! the Zephyr's my bride; if she is lost, so am I; but," he continued, drawing Ralph aside and lowering his voice still more, "this is a bad fix, Ripley; but—you've disposed of Sharp, of course?"

"Disposed of him!" growled Ralph; "he's asleep, I presume, below, taking his comfort; he must not be disturbed on any account. Probably he'd like something warm for supper."

"Tut, tut, over with him, of course; I did not calculate on this; we must not be found with _him_ on board."

"Mr. Ripley," whispered a sailor, touching him and pointing over the bow, "I think they're coming, sir."

Ralph looked and distinctly saw a dark object moving slowly and noiselessly, like a cloud on the water, and approaching the vessel in the direction of her bow, evidently to avoid danger from the guns.

"They're coming, Captain Karl," he said, "in earnest."

"*So is the wind!*" replied Sinclair, as, with one hand extended, he felt the air; "stand by to cut the cable."

"Ay, ay, sir."

In a minute more a flapping noise was heard against the masts; the next, the sails slightly filled. The order to cut was given, and the parted cable fell with a splash into the water: the canvass slowly distended, and the vessel came gracefully around, and glided, duck-like, down the bay.

Flash saw it, heard it, felt the growing breeze on his cheek, and groaned in the intensity of his anguish. A parting ball skipped past him on the wave, and he almost wished, for the moment, that it had not missed its aim.

"'Twas very hard, Captain Grim," he said, as, twenty minutes afterwards, he stood once more on shipboard, gazing gloomily seaward; "she slipped right through my fingers, sir, at the very last minute," and Flash dashed a tear from his cheek.

"Never mind, Harry," said Grim, whose usual hauteur had yielded to admiration of his young officer's valor; "never mind; Sir Henry shall hear all about it; and I'll see to your promotion myself."

This unexpected kindness came like balm to the mortified spirit of the lieutenant. He knew that Captain Grim was not lavish either of praises or promises, and he knew, moreover, that he was the brother of one of the Lords of the Admiralty. So Harry took heart, and made the best of it.

Merrily, meanwhile, went the Zephyr on her way, and as she passed slowly along near the eastern shore of the bay, the despairing Sharp gazed out from a crevice in his prison, and looked earnestly landward. He recognized, even by starlight, the shape of the coast, and knew it as his own soil, and as a part of the famed Knickerbocker manor. Long and wistfully he gazed, clinging, as it were, by his eyes, to each receding point, and looking still in the same direction when it had faded entirely from view.

Onward went the Zephyr, rapidly, merrily, and bidding a final adieu to the bay of Manhattan and all its appurtenances. Off Robins' Reef she parted with her ubiquitous Captain, who was seen the next morning leisurely smoking his *meerschaum*, as usual, on the piazza of Mynheer Schnaffenswauzer's inn.

"Flash, my fine fellow," he said, as he was accidentally joined by the lieutenant, "they tell me you had bad luck last night. I am sorry for you; I am, indeed. I always thought that—a—a —Ripton there, was a dem'd pirate; he had a bad look decidedly."

# CHAPTER XIII.

If Evert Knickerbocker's wrongs were seemingly avenged by the calamity which had befallen their author, his own condition was by no means improved. He saw his means continually decreasing, with no prospect of relief from utter poverty. He felt like the tenants of those ingenious cells of torture, the walls of which are so constructed as to move daily nearer together, until their hapless tenant is crushed between them. He saw the approach of destitution, and estimated daily its diminished distance. Ah, dreadful task! to watch the out-going stream, and the failing fountain, with no power to stay or replenish its departing tide.

But sorrows come not singly, and the venerable Evert found still another source of anxiety in the impaired health of his daughter. Not that she complained of illness, or intermitted her usual duties, but there was "*such a change*" in Effie. She, who had been so cheerful and so ready to impart courage to him, was now herself drooping, and the more evidently so, from her earnest but ineffectual attempts to maintain her former vivacity. The smile faded in its inception, the once ringing laugh was now forced and unnatural, the sparkling eyes were dimmed with frequent tears, and the pallid face was turned aside to hide them.

Her brother was the first to notice this change and to guess at its cause. The name of this young Nimrod, which is supposed to have been originally Jedediah, had been shortened by immemorial usage in the family into the initial syllable, and the very servants had no other name for him than Massa Jed. His devotion to the chase was unbounded, and it gave additional zest to the relish with which he pursued his forest sports, to know that they now contributed materially to the maintenance of the family. He was a stout, broad-shouldered young man, with the full glow of health upon features which, if none of the handsomest, possessed the inimitable charm of good nature. There was never a snarl or a crotchet visible on his face, and, let the world go as it would, he had a good word and a smile for everybody. He used to say, that next to his hounds and his hunter he loved Effie, but the truth was that his gentle sister had no rival in his affections.

During the period of Rudolph's recent visits to the Knicker-bocker family, a warm friendship had sprung up between the young men; an intimacy, indeed, of that sudden growth which could originate only between dispositions alike frank and ingenuous. They had walked, and ridden, and hunted togeth-er; and nearly all of the time which Rudolph had not devoted to Effie had been passed in the presence of her brother. Jed had, of course, suspected the sentiments of the lovers, and Effie's recent dejection had confirmed his suspicions. He felt certain that there was some unfathomed mystery in the matter, but he did not think of bestowing censure upon Rudolph, whom he knew to be the soul of sincerity and truth.

Affairs stood thus for several weeks, and Jed looked daily, but in vain, to see the returning sunshine of his sister's smile, and to hear her wonted voice of mirth welcoming him home from the woodlands. He had returned one afternoon in unusual spirits, having brought down two noble bucks after a glorious run, and he was so delighted himself that he felt sure of seeing Effie in her wonted glee. Nor was he entirely disappointed; she met him with momentary cheerfulness, for there was no resisting his contagious enthusiasm, and poor Jed rejoiced to believe that the spell was at length really broken.

"And here comes father," he shouted, as the bending form of Evert was seen moving slowly up the lawn; "two bucks, father—one with six antlers, and one ——"

But the evident abstraction of the old man and the expres-sion of his features indicating that he had something else in his thoughts, induced the son to pause.

"Rudolph is going to Holland," said Evert, as he drew nigh.

A light trembling hand was upon Jed's shoulder, and at the next moment he felt that Effie was leaning upon him for support.

"Let us go in," she said, as she slid her arm within her brother's; "the air grows cold;" and Jed, talking rapidly for her relief, accompanied her into the house.

Evert's intelligence was true. Rudolph had resolved to bid a final adieu to the province, and to seek his fortunes in his ancestral land. The pending war was rich in inducements both to patriotism and ambition, and he might bury his griefs in its turmoil, or, which seemed scarcely less desirable, terminate them in an honorable death. His Majesty's brig of war, the Terror, had been repaired, and, being on the eve of sailing, afforded him the means of proceeding at once to England, whence he could cross, if not directly to Holland, by reason of the war, yet to some part of the continent from which that country would be easily accessible.

He had one trial to endure before departing which he would gladly have avoided, and that was to bid adieu to the Knickerbockers.

Ordinary civility forbade the neglect of so obvious a duty, and a few days prior to that fixed for his departure he nerved himself to the task. Evert had both messages and packages to forward to his native land, and gladly availed himself of Rudolph's offered services to bear them. He lauded the young man's enterprise and courage, and wished him every success, not neglecting, on a momentary return of his monomania, to give one more twinge to the torture of the lover, by a repetition of his former inquiry in relation to Egbert.

Jed was not at home, and while Rudolph was talking constrainedly to Effie, the old man casually strolled away, and there was a crisis when it seemed that something must occur to dispel the singular hallucination which rested upon two ingenuous minds, each devotedly attached to the other, and yet about to separate forever. Ah! how many a term of misery has been entailed upon generous and noble hearts by some trifling misunderstanding which a word might have dispelled, and yet that word was never spoken.

If Rudolph could not fail to notice the change in Effie, he attributed it all to Egbert's perfidy, and thus the mesh of error thickened around him until he was entangled at every point.

"I fear that my father is troubling you with too many commissions," said Effie, after an embarrassing pause in conversation.

"By no means," replied Rudolph; "his letters will serve as an introduction for me, and may prove of the greatest service. Has Miss Knickerbocker no messages for her friends abroad?"

"I believe I have no friends," replied Effie, smiling faintly, "excepting father and Jed."

"It will take something from my sense of loneliness on leaving—home," said Rudolph, "if Miss Knickerbocker will allow me to believe that she includes me also in the list."

Effie bowed, and turned away, unable to speak.

There was another pause, but no good angel intervened to show this mistaken pair their folly; a formal farewell ensued—and Rudolph was gone.

## CHAPTER XIV.

The sun was approaching the western horizon, and the lengthened shadows were stretching across the waters, on the day which has last been named, when on the portico of his old Dutch mansion, walking excitedly to and fro, now pausing and muttering to himself as he looked anxiously down the road, and now resuming his rapid and noisy march, Peter Stuyvesant, ex-governor of the New Netherlands, revolved weighty matters in his mind. He was awaiting, with such patience as he could command, the return of his messenger, Hans, from the city, who, after long delay, was seen approaching at a slow walk, yet very much out of breath. Hans was no Ariel in figure, and no Puck in speed; but he was faithful and reliable to the last flicker of the feeble judgment which reposed beneath his bushy hair and his fat narrow forehead.

"Well, Hans," said the governor, when the other had recovered his breath, "have you seen them all?"

"Yaw, Mynheer," said Hans.

"Teunis, and Myndert, and Mr. Knickerbocker?"

"Yaw, Mynheer."

"And Stoutenburgh, and Poffenburgh, and Hardenburgh, and Vanderburgh?"

"Yaw, Mynheer."

"And Van Schaick, and Van Schoonhoven, and **Van Ness**, and Van Rensselaer, and Van Kortland, and Vanderpool, and Vandergrift, and Vanderveer, and Vanderspeigle?"

"Yaw——"

"And Livingston, and Schuyler, and Duyckinck, and Romaine, and Roosevelt, and Roorback, and Clapsaddle?"

Still the answer was in the affirmative.

"And are they all coming?" continued Stuyvesant, still with an excited air.

They were all coming.

"Go now, then, to Rudolph Groesbeck, and tell him that I, Peter Stuyvesant, wish to see him at my house forthwith, on private business of importance; tell it to him alone, apart, and secretly—and tell him not to speak of it; do you understand?"

"Yaw, Mynheer," said Hans; "Mr. Groesbeck musht come, and musht be mum;" and the tortoise express was again under way.

It was not long before Rudolph, not a little surprised at his singular summons, was in the presence of the governor. They were closeted together for nearly an hour, and, before their conference had ended, the congregated guests in an adjoining apartment had grown impatient for the appearance of their host. He joined them at length with little greeting, and, taking the seat which had been reserved for him, lighted his pipe and smoked for a long time in silence. The apartment was well lighted and its windows were carefully closed, and the guests, each also diligently smoking, had the air of men whose minds were by no means unoccupied. There was a look of thought and expectation on every face, and it was quite evident that no one present was ignorant of the general object of their convocation, how much soever they might be in the dark as to its particular design at that time.

Half an hour elapsed, and the clouds grew thicker, and the silence more unbroken; and frequent glances were turned, not to the governor's countenance, but to his particular pillar of smoke, to glean some indications of his sentiments, and of his approaching remarks. They were coming, evidently enough, and wrathfully, too, for the slow, graceful, and thoughtful wreaths had given place to short, quick, dense puffs which chased each other to the ceiling like miniature thunder-clouds.

"We have borne it long enough," he said at length; "we have borne it long enough."

"Long enough, Mynheer," answered Teunis Vanderbilt; and "long enough" echoed from every part of the apartment, followed by a general nodding of heads, and increased furiousness of fumigation. There were eyes, too, that gleamed like live coals through those clouds, and an under-tone of wrath ran around the room, subsiding only as the speaker resumed his address:—

"He is a tyrant, and the province is all ready to rise: Fort Orange could be ours at a moment's notice; Long Island is ripe for revolt; New Sweden is impatient for the word; and it is only here that we are powerless. But three ships of war from home would give us the city—and *we must have them.*"

Innumerable "yaw-yaws" responded to this sentiment, and the excitement rapidly increased.

"There is one of our friends," continued the speaker, with the air of a man who is about to announce a startling fact, "there is one of our friends who starts the day after to-morrow for Holland, who will carry out our dispatches, and further our designs."

4

A general and joyful surprise was manifested at this announcement, and all eyes were turned upon Yawpy Poffenburgh, who, having recently accomplished the wonderful feat of crossing the ocean, was supposed to be the only man competent to the task.

"No, no, my friends," added Stuyvesant; "here is the man," calling in Rudolph from an adjoining apartment, "young, ardent, patriotic, who stands ready to aid us—Rudolph Groesbeck, the son of my old friend and councillor, Wilhelmus."

Rudolph, thus introduced to the assembly, was received with cordial greetings, and shaking of hands, and even with tears, and great was the astonishment to learn that the studious and retired youth, whom few had known excepting by name, was brave and patriotic, and ready to venture his life in the good cause which they all had so deeply at heart. He made a few earnest remarks, assuring them of his own conviction that the time had really come when they might hope for the recovery of the province to the Dutch dominion.

"Our friends at home," he said, "are maintaining a successful war with the English; let them once know the defenceless state of this country, and the general disaffection which prevails toward the existing government, and they will send us the little help which is necessary to plant the banners of the States on yonder fort. I am ready to bear your dispatches to the home government, and to urge attention to them as best I can; and although I shall probably never revisit my native land, its welfare will ever be the object of my earnest solicitude. There is peril I know in my undertaking, but I should be spiritless indeed, if I were unwilling to encounter danger in such a cause. Let it be remembered, however, that the hazard is chiefly that of present detection. Once safely out of this port, and there is little else to fear. Be therefore, one and all, silent and discreet, and let no word or action give rise to suspicion of my errand; and above all do not come to the vessel to bid me farewell, for we have a vigilant foe, and we know not who are his agents or his spies."

Two hours before, Rudolph had been ignorant of the existence of the plot which he now so zealously espoused; but his sudden and warm advocacy of it should be no matter of surprise. It opened for him a present field of action, and would be a fitting prelude to his proposed plan of foreign service. Duty, patriotism, and ambition would under ordinary circumstances have rendered it attractive, and the prospect of a temporary oblivion of his grief was, in his unhappy state of mind, a more potent inducement still. It need scarcely be said that peril and hardship have little terror for a mind influenced by motives like these.

The venerable Evert had been a most astonished spectator and participant of this unexpected scene. "My son," he said, "have you fully considered the hazard of this enterprise? do you know that it may lead to death?"

"I do," replied Rudolph solemnly; "what great enterprise was ever accomplished without peril? But let us not fear; Heaven is ever on the side of the oppressed, and our masters, who, not content with wresting this land from its rightful owners, in a time of peace, have heaped wrongs and indignities upon us, may yet feel the edge of retribution. You, my dear sir, above all who are here, have felt the heavy hand of tyranny, and to you, above others, should the prospect of enfranchisement be welcome."

"And so it is, my dear boy, so it is," said Evert, drawing the young hero apart, as the conversation became general among the confederates; "but alas, I fear there is little to be hoped for from home. Holland is fighting against two powerful nations, and is fearfully divided in her own councils besides. We cannot shut our eyes to these facts, or expect aid from a country which may, alas, at this very moment be conquered and overrun."

"We can *try*," rejoined Rudolph, firmly, "we can try; let us at least keep up good cheer, and not injure our cause by unnecessary fears. It is natural that you, who have seen so many hopes blasted, should learn to despair; but to the young and vigorous a different duty belongs."

Evert grasped the hand of Rudolph, and tears rained from the old man's eyes as he exclaimed, "Heaven keep thee, my boy, and in better times bring thee safely back to us again."

Governor Stuyvesant proceeded next to lay before his friends a brief petition addressed to the government of the States General, setting forth the defenceless state of the province, the feasibility of its re-conquest, and its vast importance to the States, and urging their immediate action, with the promise of general co-operation on the part of the Dutch inhabitants. It was couched in concise and eloquent terms, and met with general approval; but it was left unsigned, for prudential reasons. Rudolph himself urged this as the safest course; he would feel, he said, too great responsibility if any indiscretion of his could jeopard so many valuable lives. He could sufficiently explain the names and rank and character of the petitioners to the government, and their reasons for withholding their signatures. He even proposed copying the memorial himself, lest its detection should prove fatal to poor Myndert Ten Eyck, in whose well-known crotchety characters it now appeared. "In short," he said, "if I am detected, nothing can avert my fate; but let me at least have the satisfaction of knowing that I fall alone, the first and only victim to this noble enterprise."

With an animated countenance and lofty bearing, Rudolph stood in the centre of the apartment, a young man surrounded by graybeards, eloquent in word and action, from the force of strong and natural feeling. Again they pressed around him, those venerable patriots, with congratulations and tears, overwhelmed with admiration and gratitude at his noble self-devotion. He received the petition, and was to copy it carefully, and destroy the original before going on shipboard.

He received also a plan of the harbor and channel, with the position of the fort, which had been prepared with great labor by the considerate governor, for the use of the Dutch fleet, which, in imagination, the exulting Hollanders already saw standing up the bay. This last-named document contained no writing except a few words and figures printed with a pen, which could not possibly lead to a discovery of its author. Thus armed with resources, and feeling like one to whom a mighty trust is confided, Rudolph bade his friends an affectionate farewell, and the assembly dispersed.

On the next day he was on shipboard, preparing for his departure. It was a mild, warm day, and he sat thoughtfully upon the deck, reviewing his singular position. His excitement had in a degree subsided, for the hazard was too slight, and his hoped success too remote to tell forcibly now upon his feelings; and his thoughts naturally reverted to the same dark channel in which they had previously flowed. Ah, what now, he thought, would have been his ecstasy, if he had been the possessor of Effie's love! How would he have looked forward, with all the ardor of a youthful imagination, while Fame and Wealth were thus beckoning him in the distance! How would all his lofty hopes have been blended with her dear image, all the glorious future have been radiant with her smiles!

He turned sadly from this picture, and thought of the morrow's gloom; for only one day more, and the warning song of the mariners would be heard as they raised the heavy sails, or wound the slow-moving windlass. While thus musing sadly and abstractedly, a familiar voice was in his ear, and Jed, clad in his hunting habiliments, stood before him. He had approached unobserved, in a small boat from the shore, and it was with some abatement of his usual air of cheerfulness that he extended his hand to bid his friend farewell.

"So, Ru—you are really going, eh?" he said.

"Yes," replied Ru—ruefully enough.

"Never to see New York again?"

"Never!" said Groesbeck.

"Nor your brother—nor uncle Dave?"

"No!"

"Nor father—nor me?" continued Jed.

"No, never, Jed."

"Nor—nor Snap—nor the hounds—nor Bucephalus there?" pointing with his riding-whip to his hunter, tied on the wharf.

"No," again answered Rudolph.

"Nor—nor Effie?" continued Jed at length, eyeing his companion closely, but with seeming carelessness.

Rudolph turned pale, and, despite his most strenuous efforts at composure, his voice faltered as he replied:

"No, my dear fellow, never—never."

Jed required no further proof of suspicion which had before nearly amounted to certainty.

"You're sure you're doing right, I suppose, Rudolph?" he continued, after a pause, and slashing the deck meanwhile with his whip.

"I believe that I am," replied Groesbeck, with surprise; "at all events, I leave but few behind me who are interested in my fate."

"Rudolph," rejoined Jed, still looking deckward and whipping the planks, "I have not come to you with any message or mission, or with the knowledge of any one. I am, as you see, on my way to the forest, and yonder, even now, goes old Jake with the hounds. But I have turned aside—Ru—to bid you farewell, and to ask you if you are sure, quite sure—Ru—that you are doing right?"

"There is some hidden meaning in your words, Jed," replied Rudolph, hurriedly and hoarsely; "speak plainly, quickly, for the love of Heaven!"

"I will," said Jed; "Effie——"

"Yes——" exclaimed Rudolph.

"Effie——"

"Yes," was again the eager response.

"I cannot tell you, Ru; she would die if she thought I had spoken to you. She has never said or hinted a word to me; but I can *see*, Rudolph, and I fear you are laboring under some dreadful mistake," and Jed slashed the poor deck more unmercifully than ever.

"Does she care aught for me?" asked Groesbeck, quickly, and seizing the hand of his companion with the grasp of a vice; "does she not love Egbert—expect—hope for his return?"

"That she never loved Egbert—that she loathes him now—that she does not expect or desire his return—that the wealth of worlds could not induce her to smile upon him—all this I *know*," replied Jed; "that she cares for you, Rudolph, it is hardly proper for me to say; but she used to be happy in your presence, and now she is——but I have said enough, Ru—too much perhaps, so——good bye."

"Wait a minute," exclaimed Groesbeck, starting in three several directions in a breath, and each time coming back to the same spot; "wait a minute, Jed;—halloo there, you, Jack! Jim! Joe!" calling down below and summoning to the gangway the apparition of a woolly-headed waiter, with a frightened aspect; "I'm going on shore, Bill," he said; "take care of my boxes there you know—come along Jed—and halloo there—don't sail, you know, till I come back."

The white eyes of the negro expanded over the sable disc of his face like the passing off of an eclipse; "Golly, massa," he said, "*I* can't stop her."

"Oh, very true, Sam," said Rudolph, whose thoughts, revolving in a whirl of excitement, were fairly jumbled together: "very true," he said, for at that moment he caught a glimpse of three distinct ideas as they flitted by—the first of which was that the negro was not the captain; the second, that the vessel would not wait three seconds for him in any event; and the third, that she was not to sail till the next day, and that he would therefore have ample time to get back before her departure, without the aid of seven-league boots. "So, come along, Jed," he exclaimed once more, and the friends departed together.

The events which immediately ensued scarcely require to be narrated. Jed did not accompany his friend to his father's home, and Effie, while walking in the garden,

" Its fairest flowers eclipsed by her,"

beheld Rudolph approaching, and anticipated with dread another painful interview. But there was a new strange look on his flushed features, and he called her "Effie." The " Terror " was lying within their view, and, at Rudolph's instance, they strolled toward the river that they might see it the more plainly. There stood the latticed arbor, and loitering, embarrassedly, half within it, to adjust a fallen vine, Effie's little hand has been taken gently captive, and pressed to burning lips, and warm and fervent words of love, of pure and holy love, are murmured in her ear. The whole story of his alternating hopes and fears, of his single-hearted and truthful affection, has been told and repeated, but has not been answered.

No word has spoken approval, and no look has betokened it —but the little hand is unwithdrawn and the half-averted face, and the drooping lids, and the one trembling tear are more eloquent than words. There are scenes and sentiments which should be left undesecrated by pen or pencil, and which only the Daguerrean power of the Imagination can portray. Smile ye who will, but pure and passionless affection is no chimera of the mind. The fountain in the desert—the flower on the heath —a star in the clouded sky ; these are its images, and its types as far as mortal objects can adumbrate immortality.

## CHAPTER XV.

On that memorable evening when the conclave at Governor Stuyvesant's was in session, a single horseman, casually passing the house, had his attention arrested by the singular appearance of the light bursting through the chinks and crannies of the closed blinds, in the room which all New York knew to be the governor's best parlor. The equestrian gazed a little while, wonderingly, and was about to pass on, when the dismissed party came pouring out of the front doorway, uttering many a loud "good night" to their host, who, candle in hand, watched them down the lawn.

It was a dark evening, lighted faintly by the stars, and there were shadowy spots on the way-side, beneath overhanging trees, which were darker still. Into one of these the rider reined his horse, and, unobserved, awaited the approach of the party. Their nodding heads and whispering voices and vehement gestures conveyed no other idea to the listener than the addition of some new ghost to the spirit family of the island, whose advent was the subject of comment, and whose assaults were to be avoided by clustering closely together. But the frequent mention of Rudolph's name, and the appearance of one slight and erect form, towering above the bended figures of his companions, excited no little surprise. A party of old Dutch gentlemen at the governor's was no unusual occurrence, but what was young Groesbeck doing in such an assemblage?

Thus wondering, though only with the curiosity of an idle mind, and attaching no importance to the occurrence, the horseman waited until the party had passed, and then resumed his way. It has been said that there was starlight only, and that of the faintest kind, but, feeble as were the celestial rays, they would have revealed to the most careless observer, in the proportions of the rider, in his position and motions, and in the general *Benhadadity* of his air, the person of the junior Sharp. But Benhadad was not Hiram, or no bubble had been too frail, no brushed cobweb too evanescent, to emblem the brilliant scheme on which so many hopes were hung.

Yet when on the second ensuing day, mingling with the crowd who thronged to see the departure of the "Terror,"

Sharp heard for the first time, that Rudolph was on board, a passenger to England, a slow, dull, tedious process of ratiocination began to take place in his brain, confusedly connecting the event with the circumstances of which he had so lately been a witness. At times he seemed to catch the glimpse of an idea beyond the isolated facts, and to wonder whether there was not something strange in it, and then, with much chuckling at his sagacity, he resolved to mention the matter to Governor Lovelace—the very first time that he should meet that officer.

In the mean time, many anxious hearts were watching the embarkation. From the long Dutch stoop of Evert Knickerbocker; from the terrace of Anthony Ten Broeck; from the distant windows of the Van Schaicks and Van Tassels, the Van Bummels and Van Pelts, old heads and spectacled eyes were peering; and whispering voices asked, and whispered words replied that all seemed safe and quiet yet. They had regarded Rudolph's prudent injunctions in remaining at home, but painful indeed was their suspense.

Rudolph himself was not free from fear. His new hopes, the bliss which had so suddenly deluged his heart, had increased by a thousandfold his value of life; and the perils which he had held so lightly before seemed now of no trivial magnitude. It was not now as an exile that he was about to quit his native shores, but as a patriot, bound on a lofty mission, and looking forward to a speedy return and a happy reunion with the friends whom he left behind. Not that he shrunk from encountering peril, or would have abated aught from the glorious enterprise to which he had pledged his exertions; but it was with a fast beating heart that he watched the slow processes of raising the heavy anchors, and setting the ample sails. The musical chorus of the sailors, as they bent cheerily to their tasks, became harsh and discordant sounds to his excited nerves, and his suspense was increased by his inability to judge of the point of progress attained in these mysterious operations.

Benhadad continued an interested spectator of the scene, and as the affair of Rudolph continued to occur at intervals to his mind, he looked around for some one to whom he might mention his thoughts. But seeing no one in the undistinguished throng around him, worthy of his confidence, he again wrapped himself in his dignity, in which very comfortable envelope he bade fair to remain inclosed, until after the departure of the vessel.

But the anchor is well nigh in—the sails are nearly set—the last boat is hoisted up, and swings, dangling, like a toy, at

4*

the vessel's side, and noble hearts beat freer, and aching eyes grow less vigilant in the distance.

"Ah, Sharp, my dear friend, how are you?" said a mild bland voice in Benhadad's ear: "a fine vessel, isn't she? I understand our ruralizing, botanizing, contemplative. poetical friend, young Groesbeck, goes out—eh? where the deuce is he going to?"

"See here, Captain Sinclair!" exclaimed Benhadad, now burning with his pent secret; and, drawing his companion aside, he whispered earnestly for some moments in his ear, during which period the captain's countenance underwent some singular changes. "I dare say," concluded the informant, "there's nothing in it, of course, you know—but then—it's queer, isn't it?"

"Blinds closed—all Dutchmen—Rudolph the only young man present—and he now starting off mysteriously in the Terror—war raging between Holland and England," repeated Sinclair, touching at once on the prominent points; "why, here is no *suspicion*, man; here is *certainty!*"—and before Benhadad could reply his companion had vanished.

"It's strange what a confounded hurry he's in," muttered Benhadad, as he again gave himself up to a contemplation of the majestic vessel, which now came gracefully around, and, with distended sails, stood gallantly down the bay.

Then came the flash, the smoke, the loud reverberation of the parting salute, the prompt response from the fort, the merry cheers, and waving hats, and signs of last adieu. Steadily onward, slowly at first, but more briskly soon, she passes on her way, leaving town and fort behind; and the banners of St. George are fluttering at her peak, and the merry troll of the mariners comes more faintly to the ear, and long, deep breaths are drawn by fervent hearts on shore, and hopes are growing brighter, and grateful tears are shed.

Half an hour elapsed, but the gaping crowd did not disperse. Some new commotion has arrested the general gaze. Messengers were seen passing rapidly to and from the government house; signals were flying from the fort; the governor himself, accompanied by Captain Sinclair, made his appearance, and walked hastily to the battery, and strange whisperings of unintelligible events prevailed. Presently the guns of the fort were fired in quick succession, and, after considerable delay, a sail-boat, darting out into the stream, went racing down the bay, in the wake of the Terror. A hundred hearts stood still, but onward went the ship. In vain did the echoing cannon continue to thunder from the fort; they were regarded only as repetitions

of the parting salute, and as such were from time to time replied
to by the guns of the vessel.  The signals were either not seen,
or not understood, and all the alternating hopes and fears of the
spectators soon centred upon the relative speed of the messen-
ger-boat and its leviathan chase.

Had the wind been fresh, the ship, with its towering cloud of
canvass, would doubtless soon have passed from view; but the
breeze, while strong enough to give the feathery little bark a
rapid headway, told of course less effectually upon its bulky com-
petitor.  Yet the difference of speed was too slight to admit of
making any certain calculations upon the result.  A stern chase
is proverbially a long one, and the waterman who guided the
little craft had been dispatched, in the hurry of the hour, unpro-
vided with the means of making any conspicuous signals.

Rudolph stood meanwhile upon the quarter-deck of the Terror,
a prey to the most harrowing anxiety.  With a sagacity sharpened by the danger which surrounded him, he had at once conjectured the cause of the commotion on shore, and he watched
with fearful interest the progress of the pursuing boat.  His first
impulse was to destroy the papers which might prove such fearful evidence against him; but their importance to the success of
his mission was such that he resolved to defer their destruction
until more certain of its necessity.  He thought that his fears
might magnify the danger; that the pursuit might be for some
other object, and that, at all events, there would be abundant
opportunity for such a purpose before any one authorized either
to arrest or examine him could board the vessel, for the present
pursuer was clearly enough no officer of justice.

Concealing his trepidation as best he could, he awaited the
course of events, and, to avoid directing attention to the sail-
boat, was obliged to content himself with only occasional and
furtive glances in that direction.  Lieutenant Flash joined him
and rallied him upon his low spirits: "Just so myself," he said,
"the first time I went to sea—all right, sir—you'll be sea-sick
by-and-by, and then you'll feel better; but halloo! what's this?"
he continued, as, looking off toward the harbor, he caught sight
of the sail in their wake: "why, Groesbeck, she's chasing us,
making signals, and all that; she is, indeed; there must be
something wrong;" and the lieutenant was about to transmit
the intelligence to the Captain, when he felt the hand of Rudolph upon his shoulder, and turning around, saw the pale face
of his companion looking earnestly at him.

"Mr. Flash," he said, "do you believe me to be guilty of any
crime deserving of death?"

"*You! crime! death!*" replied Flash rapidly; "why, no, sir,
of course not.  I know better."

"Look this way, then," said Rudolph, whisperingly; "I cannot tell you now what I mean; but do not look at that boat; do not point your glass toward her—for it is probable that my life depends upon her not overtaking us."

"What—what—what?" said Flash hastily, and laying down his glass; "is it so?" and turning from Rudolph, he issued a succession of rapid orders, which were as rapidly obeyed by the sailors, and another snowy sail capped the pyramidal canvas that rose above the decks of the Terror. "The Captain and First are at dinner yet," he said, turning again to Rudolph, "and will be for the next half hour. There is no one else to fear; in twenty minutes we'll be outside of the Hook; so never fear, my good sir, never fear."

Rudolph grasped the hand of his companion, and thanked him with such voice as his choked utterance would permit.

"No, no, never mind," said Flash; "I know you didn't do it, no matter what it was—confound the bailiffs, and all that; now we go, sir—isn't that a dashing speed?"

And onward sped the Terror, rising and sinking to the long, heavy swell which proclaimed the open sea to be close at hand. Ten minutes elapsed, and the ocean gate, widening to their nearer view, revealed the white crested waves beyond, chasing each other "like snowy coursers on the race."

"She'll scarcely venture outside in such a sea as that," said Flash: "courage, my friend. Ah, if it would only blow great guns now, there wouldn't be a speck of danger; I think it *does* come a little fresher"—feeling the air with his hand; and thus the good-natured Lieutenant ran on, attempting to encourage his companion, but delicately abstaining from any inquiries into the particular cause of his alarm. He knew enough, however, of the hostility of the Dutch inhabitants of New York to the existing government, to suspect that Groesbeck's offence, if any, was of a political character, and if so, there were obvious reasons just at that moment why the Lieutenant should prefer to remain uninformed of it. A brief acquaintance with Rudolph on shore had convinced him that the latter could not be justly chargeable with the obloquy of any personal crime.

"She gains on us a little, I think," said Rudolph, casting a hasty glance behind.

"Never mind," replied Flash, "here we are in the very portals of the sea—she'll vanish here, like a ghost at the church-yard;" and onward rushed the ship, with a momentarily increasing motion—her speed being now rendered more apparent by the rapidly shifting objects on the adjacent land. The very sound of the breakers on the nearest shore came distinctly to the ear, and the sparkling waves could be seen chasing each other sportively up the beach. A few minutes more, and the shores were rapidly receding, and a boundless waste of waters was opening to the view.

"Good bye—good bye, my little friend," exclaimed Flash exultingly; "unless you see fit to cross the Atlantic with us, in which case you had better——"

"Mr. Flash!" exclaimed a startling voice from the cabin gangway, "*yonder is a small boat following us and making signals; slacken sail a little, and let her come up.*"

It was the voice of fate, and could not be gainsayed. The vanishing head of Captain Grim was just seen as he again disappeared in the cabin, and the Lieutenant, directing a deprecatory glance toward Rudolph, issued the necessary orders, and in half an hour the boat was alongside. Rudolph's heart sank within him, but summoning his resolution, he awaited the *dénouement* with such composure as he could command. He still indulged the hope that his apprehensions had been needlessly excited, and that the errand of the boat had no reference to himself. How, indeed, could his secret have transpired at the very moment of his departure? Surely his excitement and anxiety had conjured up a phantom of danger where none in reality existed. He would not yet destroy his papers, which were carefully concealed within the lining of one of his travelling boxes, for there could be no lack of opportunity for that purpose, if it became necessary to accomplish it.

Alas! he had little calculated on the cruel sagacity of his foes. The sail-boat came alongside, and a sealed note for Captain Grim was passed into the ship. The surprised air with which he perused it—his glance at Rudolph, and his instantaneous orders for a return to port, left little room for hope; but when, a few minutes subsequently, Rudolph attempted to pass below, and found himself interdicted, he at length knew the worst.

"Mr. Groesbeck will excuse me," said Captain Grim, "for requesting him to remain where he now is, until we return to port; some suspicions, groundless I hope, are entertained, and I am requested to forbid you access to your luggage, until it can be searched by an officer of justice."

The request was of course a command, and Rudolph, whose native courage and fortitude now came to his aid, quietly acquiesced. He soon became conscious even that he was closely watched to prevent the destruction of any papers which he might have about his person.

The sad details of events immediately ensuing need scarcely

be related. Let it suffice to know that when, a few hours subsequently, the spreading sails of the Terror once more faded to a cloud within the distant Narrows, Rudolph Groesbeck was not upon her decks. Guarded, manacled, the tenant of a felon's cell, he awaited a speedy trial for the crime of High Treason against the majesty of Charles the Second.

## CHAPTER XVI.

AVALANCHE-LIKE, in its force and impetuosity, had been the descent of this dreadful calamity; and if anything could add aggravation to the blow, it was a contemplation of the contemptible means by which it had been effected. The mountain had been undermined by a mouse. The discomfited confederates needed no summons to bring them together on the evening of that memorable day; one by one, as the shadows of twilight deepened, did they wend their lonely way to the distant Bowery, hoping to gain from their leader the encouragement which their own hearts failed to afford. But all regret for their vanished hopes of conquest were lost sight of for the present, in view of the appalling fate which impended over their young and chivalrous ally.

There was no view of the affair which presented any semblance of hope in his behalf. He was in the hands of a rigorous government, bound by the principle of self-preservation to suppress every form of insurrection, and to crush each embryo bud of treason. They knew that even a mild and moderate government might plausibly have punished Rudolph's offence with death, and that from the despotic tribunal of Lovelace no leniency in such a case could be expected. Some fears for their own safety mingled with these apprehensions, and altogether it was a gloomy congress which convened on that dismal evening at the house of Governor Stuyvesant.

Governor Stuyvesant growled like a chained lion, but he indulged in no idle vaunts. A blank despair, indeed, pervaded the whole council, and while many schemes for relief were revolved, each was in turn abandoned as utterly hopeless. It was resolved, however, that immediate measures should be taken to learn the designs of the government, and, if any fair trial was to be allowed to the accused, no pains were to be spared in furnishing him with skilful counsel, and such other aid as might be practicable. Having designated a few of their number to obtain the earliest possible information on the subject, the assembly dispersed to meet again on the ensuing evening, unless some exigency should call them sooner together.

There was no one who said less, or endured more on this try-

ing occasion, than Mr. Knickerbocker. He felt as if all Rudolph's sufferings were in some way traceable to himself, and it
seemed as if the impending tragedy was to be the crowning
calamity of his life. That he passed a weary night, finding sleep
without repose and dreams more fatiguing than toil, need scarcely
be said. On the ensuing morning, he was early abroad, seeking
to glean such information as he could find upon the subject
which now engrossed his whole attention. His steps were
naturally directed toward the jail in which Rudolph was confined, which stood closely adjoining the fort, and fronting toward
the Hudson river at a point very near the southern extremity of
the city. Near to that gloomy tenement he saw, sauntering, one
of those grim officials of the law, who execute its most odious
and repulsive decrees without even the show of reluctance. Hid-
ing a cruel and sanguinary disposition under the guise of devotion
to his official duty, Hugh Gore, at once the jailer and executioner
of the city, added, by the natural ferocity of his look and manner, increased intensity to every punishment which he inflicted.
In vain did the prisoner, newly arrested, look into his face for
some gleam of encouragement or sympathy. The very act of
turning the prison bolts was performed with an emphasis which
betokened a relish of the welcome sound; and if the victim was
one, the accusation against whom was of a capital nature, he
would be sure to be favored by Hugh with a cell which com-
manded a full view of the permanent gallows, scarcely less lofty
than that of Haman, which, to the disgrace of the infant city,
then formed one of its prominent features.

To this ogre, the timid and child-like Evert applied courte-
ously for information as to the situation of his young friend, and
the nature of the charges against him.

"Charges?" said Hugh, sardonically; "oh, nothing, I believe,
more than high treason, and some such little matters; 'tisn't
anything, you know, to invite the king's enemies into the country, and offer to help them overturn the government—that ain't
anything, is it, old fellow?"

"When is he to be tried?" rejoined Evert, with difficulty sup-
pressing his emotion.

"There are older heads than his in this business," replied
Hugh, not heeding the question, "if we can only get at them;
some fine estates to be confiscated, too. You don't know anything about it though, I dare say; and then some folks's estates
are out of all danger of confiscation—ha! ha! ha!—you can't get
two skins off one cat—ho! ho! ho!" and an echoing laugh from
within told that Hugh was not talking for his own edification
alone.

"Can you tell me when Mr. Groesbeck is to be tried?" repeated Evert mildly, and still repressing all signs of indignation at the brutality of his companion.

"Tried, quotha?" returned Hugh; "tried? no, not exactly; but there is a man," pointing across the street, toward a shop of miscellaneous cabinet-ware, "there's a man in that shop who can tell you something about it, I reckon;" and so saying, Hugh retired within doors, whence still the jeering laugh came back to Evert's ears.

The old man directed his steps slowly across the road to the place which had been designated by his informant, and, in the simplicity of his heart, applied with the same inquiry to a workman whom he found busily engaged within.

"Rudolph Groesbeck? when is he to be tried, do you ask?" said the carpenter respectfully, pausing meanwhile from his work, and leaning on the end of his plane.

"Yes, sir," returned Mr. Knickerbocker, glad that he seemed like to meet with no further insults; "the jailer told me he thought you could inform me when his trial would take place."

The man looked curiously and sympathizingly into old Evert's anxious face, and then gave a quick, furtive glance toward the opposite side of his shop as he replied: "I don't know exactly when he's to be tried—pretty soon, I should reckon—*that's for him;*" and Evert's eyes, following the direction pointed out by his companion, fell upon a newly made and freshly stained coffin.

Leaning, clinging to the lintel of the doorway, pale, trembling, gasping, Mr. Knickerbocker in vain essayed for some moments to speak.

"For him?" he said at length; "for *Rudolph Groesbeck?* it is impossible; by whose orders has this been done?"

"Oh, Hugh sees to all these things; he ordered it. I guess it's all right, sir—he don't often make a mistake about such matters."

"The hard-hearted scoundrel—the fiend!" exclaimed the old man.

"No, no," said the carpenter, "I wouldn't call hard names—it ain't always safe. He gives me a good many jobs, Hugh does, but he is rather hasty, I think myself, at times; he sometimes measures his men for these things as soon as he gets 'em inside, sir. When you've got a thing to do, then do it, and don't be puttin' off things—that's Hugh's maxim."

"But Rudolph has not been convicted or even tried yet—much less sentenced to death."

"Wal, p'raps not; I don't know much about these things; but that won't take long, I reckon. I hearn something said about a court to be held this afternoon at the Stadt-Huys, as soon as the

races are over—may be that's it;" and the workman resumed his
labors with a rapidity which manifested a disposition at once to
put an end to the colloquy, and to make amends for the time
which had already been consumed upon it.

With a heavy heart and tottering steps did Evert return to his
house, where for a while he yielded to the most bitter and hopeless despair. To Jed, who was equally appalled at his friend's
danger, and ready to do anything in his behalf, he at once imparted the alarming facts which he had learned, and entreated
him to hasten to Governor Stuyvesant with the intelligence.

"Tell him," he said, "that if anything can be done, it must be
immediately; to-morrow may be too late."

Jed hastened to execute his mission, tarrying only to enjoin
upon his father that he should withhold from Effie all knowledge
of these dreadful facts, for she was entirely ignorant of the impending calamity. She knew nothing even of Rudolph's arrest;
and her heart continued glad, as watching the favoring skies she
anticipated his prosperous voyage and safe return.

Stuyvesant received Jed's information with but little surprise.
"Yes, yes," he said, "they'll murder the poor fellow of course,
and we have got to sit still and look tamely on; but go, and learn
with certainty the time and place of his trial; we will at least
behold the mockery, and do all for him that we can."

But the necessity for haste did not prove to be as great as had
been anticipated. The executioner's cruel orders had been altogether gratuitous, and were entirely unknown to Governor Lovelace. The latter, indeed, could not be chargeable with a sanguinary disposition; yet, in the ever rigorous discharge of his
official trust, clemency was not to be looked for at his hands.
His very hostility to the Dutch inhabitants had resulted more
from a knowledge of their disloyalty to the existing powers than
from any personal ill-will toward them. Faithful to his own
master, he was still not capable of giving them credit for fidelity
to the States, nor mindful of the steps of doubtful equity by which
the latter had been divorced from their long-cherished colonies.

The principal judicial tribunal which existed at this time in
the province was called the Court of Assize, and was composed
of the governor himself and two or three justices of the peace.
Although created by no legislative enactment, but organized by
Lovelace in pursuance of the plenary powers with which he was
invested, it possessed perhaps sufficient authority to arraign and
try the accused. But desirous to attach more weight to the affair, and to imitate in some respect the formula of State trials
in England, the governor issued a special commission of oyer and
terminer for this purpose to one Sir Thomas Colton and two justices of the peace, and an interval of six days was allowed to
elapse previous to the trial.

Rudolph was also informed that he would be allowed the benefit of counsel, and that if he had any witnesses in his behalf they should be heard. There was something, however, in all this ceremony which seemed like a mere show of clemency, where the substance was wanting. It seemed indeed to Rudolph's despairing mind a sort of challenge and defiance, as if he had been told that he should have every opportunity of defence for the very purpose of demonstrating the hopeless certainty of his guilt, and the justice of his coming condemnation.

It would be painful and unnecessary to dwell upon the interval of suspense which intervened prior to the sitting of the court, or to depict the sad details of the trial. Rudolph's deportment was dignified and calm, but there was an expression of anguish at times upon his face, which spoke of suffering beyond any that the fear of death had power to inflict. His own suddenly blasted hopes, the pain and degradation of an ignominious execution, were scarcely present to his mind; but who shall tell the agony of his soul as he contemplated the impending misery of her, who, still unconscious of his danger, was yet to meet the full shock of so overwhelming a grief.

Every effort was made in his behalf, but all was in vain. The proof admitted of no denial. The papers which had been found in his possession told the whole story of his culpability; and the fact of their careful concealment among his luggage gave confirmation to the proof. The eloquent petition, the accurate plan of the harbor and channel, the private letters of Mr. Knickerbocker, which, although containing no allusion to political subjects, showed the intended destination of their bearer, were all produced and commented on, carrying conviction to the minds of the hearers. Rudolph in short was found guilty, and, when asked, with the usual formula of the law, whether he had anything to say why sentence should not be pronounced against him, he remained silent. Not even when demanded a second time did he essay to reply, until, answering rather the appealing looks of his friends than the voice of the judge, he briefly addressed the court.

"If aught," he said, "if aught that I can allege could serve to avert or palliate a doom which I dread less for myself than others, I might indeed say something against my impending sentence. I might speak of political wrongs sought to be righted; of duty which is counted crime, and patriotism stigmatized as treason; but I could neither deny my acts, nor repudiate the principles which prompted them. I know that I must die—ignominiously—on the scaffold,"—his voice faltered as he spoke—"but I die a martyr and not a criminal."

He sat down, and a shudder ran through the audience as the presiding judge, with the judicial ceremony of the age, assumed the black cap which betokened the sentence of death. With dignified composure, yet not without feeling, was his official duty discharged. He spoke of the imperative obligation incumbent upon ministers of justice to punish those crimes which aimed at the subversion of government, and remarked upon the peculiar situation of the province, endangered by enemies from abroad, and by disaffection at home, as a reason for the most rigid enforcement of the law.

He then proceeded to sentence the prisoner, fixing the third ensuing day for his execution, and warning him not to indulge the faintest hope of pardon or reprieve. The court then adjourned, and Rudolph, in the clutch of the gratified Hugh, was remanded to his cell. What bitter tears were shed, what noble hearts were wrung, how voiceless with grief his faithful friends crowded around him, seeking vainly to give some word of cheer, need not be related. Petition and remonstrance were all in vain; the governor remained inexorable, and even hinted at further prosecutions if the least additional provocation were given.

If there was one of Rudolph's friends who now suffered more than the rest, it was Jed; on whom plainly devolved a task scarcely less dreadful than that of suffering side by side with his friend; for from his lips must Effie receive the appalling tidings which should prepare her once more to meet Rudolph, and then to part with him forever.

## CHAPTER XVII

THE city jail, as has been described, stood near the fort, and fronting toward the Hudson, at a point near the confluence of that stream with the East River. A little to the north, on the same street, was the governor's house, a large, but in no way ostentatious building, and immediately adjacent, but fronting in another direction, was the old Dutch Church. A narrow court-yard intervened between the jail and the street, and a long stoop, the invariable accompaniment of Dutch buildings, extended the whole width of the house. Upon this stoop, on the evening which succeeded to that melancholy day, the events of which have just been related, sat Hugh Gore, wrapt in no unpleasing contemplations.

The sun had gone down; the lingering twilight was growing gradually less; and the light sea-breeze, setting landward, was lifting the shaggy locks of the jailer, as gently as if they had been the curls of cradled innocence. Musing deeply and alone, and watching with complacent countenance the thin wreaths which curled slowly upward from his pipe, he was aroused from his reverie by the heavy tread of some one passing in the street.

On looking up, he saw a man clad in a thin spencer and wide-legged trowsers, and wearing the glazed tarpaulin which then as now was a distinctive badge of the fraternity of sailors. He had passed Hugh apparently without noticing him, but turning suddenly back, and exhibiting by the movement the neck of a glass bottle protruding from his outer pocket, he touched his hat civilly and inquired the way to a well-known dram-shop in the neighborhood.

"Huyck's?" said Hugh, good-naturedly; "why, you must be a stranger here if you don't know where Huyck's is, and you a sailor, too!"

"I am," replied the other, again touching his hat, "and have just come from Boston in the Dolly—yonder she lies, with the blue bunting. Will your honor please to tell me——"

"Oh, yes," said Hugh, giving the desired direction; "but don't go and spend all your money like a fool."

The sailor smiled, and, thanking his informant, passed on, and Gore, wrapt in his peculiar reflections, had quite forgotten the incident, when, a few minutes afterwards, it was recalled to his mind by a return of the stranger. He seemed now slightly affected by the atmosphere of Mynheer Huyck's tap-room, and disposed to be social and communicative; and, after bandying merry phrases with Hugh for a few minutes, he produced his bottle, and invited his companion to drink. The jailer sniffed daintly at the cork, prepared to utter a sneer at the vile whiskey, or at some compound still viler, though bearing a more ambitious name, when he became conscious that his olfactories were regaled with the fumes of a liquor, rare and costly at that period in the province, and highly prized by the epicurean race.

"The de'il," he exclaimed, applying his huge nose again and again to the mouth of the bottle; "is it possible that Huyck sells genuine Jamaica, and that sailors buy it? Walk up, Mr. Jack Tar, walk up, and take a seat, while I get some cups, and we'll have a taste of its quality."

The sailor needed no second bidding, and, taking a seat on the stoop, awaited the return of the other from within, who soon made his appearance with some drinking utensils, and then led the way to a part of the piazza less exposed to view from the street, for he was in no way desirous of attracting any additional guests to so rare a banquet. Smacking his lips over his cup, he needed but little urging to renew again and again the delicious potation.

The sailor was exceedingly merry, and had many a jovial tale to tell, which, whatever their real merits, grew more and more amusing to his auditor; who finally swore, upon the winding up of a long story about crossing the line, and being shaved by father Neptune with an iron hoop, that his particular friend, Mr. Jack Tar, was the very pink of sailors, and he really hoped, upon his soul and body, that he never should be called upon to do any little unpleasant jobs in the way of stringing up or cutting down so choice a fellow.

"Stringing up and cutting down," repeated the sailor, who despite his seemingly large draughts preserved a tolerable appearance of sobriety; "what do you mean by that, Mr. Gore?"

"I mean," replied Hugh, with an involuntary twinkle of his eye, "that I am grand Bashaw here, with nine tails—there they hang, up there," pointing to a huge instrument of flagellation, reposing above their heads; "and also, that I tend that guide-post to the Future State out there," pointing to the gallows, which in the gloom of the evening loomed up to an unusual altitude before them.

Hugh did not notice the shudder which shook for a moment

the frame of his companion, any more than he had noticed the dozen discarded draughts which the other had slyly spilled into the garden, over the railing against which his chair was leaning.

"Oh, ho, you are the executioner, then?" returned the sailor; "probably you run up that Growsbeck, then, that was hung the other day, for treason."

"No, sir," replied Gore, with a chuckle; "he hain't been hung yet, Mr. Groesbeck hain't: I expect the melancholy pleasure of turning him off the day after to-morrow, at nine o'clock, and shall be very happy of your presence on that occasion—a large company expected—front seats reserved for the ladies;" and Hugh laughed at his hideous joke.

"He's a desperate hard case, I suppose; I should like wonderfully to see him—you don't know where they keep him, I suppose?"

"Don't know?" returned Hugh; "maybe I don't—if I don't know, who does?—that's it. See here, my salt-water friend, do you see them winders there, with fancy lattice work across them? well, that's the jail, and in there's the onfortinet man; and in here," striking his jingling pocket with his hand, "in here are the keys that keep him there."

Mr. Gore's guest expressed no little surprise at these pieces of information, and reiterating his desire to see so awful a criminal, Hugh at length volunteered to gratify his wishes and conduct him within. The jailer's step as he rose for this purpose was by no means steady, and Jed, for he, as may have been conjectured, was the assumed sailor, seemed to be equally under the effects of the bottle.

It was no easy matter for the inebriated man to apply his ponderous key, and open the prison door, but after much fumbling and muttering that difficult feat was accomplished, and, the door being left slightly ajar, the companions passed in. There was a principal central room, which was usually occupied by offenders of the lesser grades, and off this apartment were several cells designed for such malefactors as needed especial guarding. But as Gore had at this time no other persons under his charge, and Rudolph's appearance had excited no apprehensions of any very desperate attempt at escape, he had allowed the prisoner the benefit of the larger room; not, however, without the precaution of chaining him by one foot to a ring in the floor. This chain was secured by a padlock, the key to which Hugh also carried in his pocket.

"There he is—there he is," exclaimed Gore, speaking thickly, for the liquor was taking effect more fully upon his brain; "look at him quick, Mr. Tar, and then let's go back, for there'll be some one else here to see him soon, I dare say, but nobody's to come in to-night without the governor's orders, except Dominie Megapolensis."

So saying, the jailer took a seat near the door, while Jed approached his friend, who was sitting on a rude wooden chair, with his face turned to the wall, and with his head resting upon his hands. There was a dim light in the room, left rather by the stinted grace of the keeper than as a matter of right.

"See what luxuries he has," muttered Hugh, with his chin dropping upon his breast—"lights and a seat, and a large room all to himself—'tisn't everybody gets such treatment, and he wouldn't, you know, only his time is short."

The prisoner had turned partly around upon the entrance of the visitors, but, after a momentary glance at them, quietly resumed his former position. Jed approached him slowly, talking meanwhile to the keeper in his assumed manner, but as he came nearer he contrived, parenthetically, to pronounce Rudolph's name in his natural voice, and in a low tone. A quick nervous motion of the prisoner ensued; he raised his head slightly, and was about to speak, when his friend's fingers rested upon his lips, and he remained silent. But from that moment every faculty was alive.

"You've got him chained, eh?" said Jed; "that's right—I see you know how to make sure of such fellows; bolts, bars, and chains—you understand it, don't you, Mr. Gore?"

"Of course I do," growled Hugh.

"And yet you are merciful too, considering," said Jed.

"Certainly," said Gore—"see that chair, and candle—and—and cup of water."

"Yes, certainly; but now it's my opinion, Mr. Jailer, that that chain is a little too tight, and that it hurts the poor fellow's ankle; you don't want to keep him in pain, I know; I'd jest shift it to t'other leg, and make it a trifle looser."

There is said to be no safer or more acceptable flattery than that which gives an individual credit for the quality which of all others he most lacks, and it must have been on this principle that Jed had attributed the heavenly virtue of Mercy to his brutal companion. Evidently flattered by the remark, the now stolid keeper came forward and inquired of Rudolph if the fetters were painful.

"He *says* that they hurt him," replied Jed, hastening to speak for the other, "and any one can see that it is so; it will be but a moment's work to shift the chain to the other leg."

"Oh yes," said Hugh, "I can do it in a twinkling, but let me jes lock the door first, because a man in his case gets dreadful desperate sometimes, and he might make a rush, and get away from us, you know."

"Oh, I'll see to that," exclaimed Jed; and skipping past the jailer he transferred the key from the outer to the inner side, and, shutting the door, locked it, but without removing the key.

Satisfied that all was now safe, and that his prisoner, however daring, could do nothing against the combined efforts of himself and the sailor, Gore stooped and unlocked the chain—removed it from one leg of Rudolph, and was about transferring it to the other, when he found himself suddenly lying upon his back, with Jed astride of his body, and a strong hand at his throat.

"If you speak you will die," said Jed, firmly; "if you are quiet you shall not be harmed—do you understand?"

Purple with fright and suffocation, Hugh winked in reply, for, pinioned and throttled as he was, it was the only gesture he could make; and Jed, who had not come unprepared for his work, produced some stout cords and a gag, with which, in a few moments, the helpless jailer was secured beyond the power of speech or motion. The chain was next applied to his huge leg and securely locked, and the young men, trembling with intense excitement, were hastening toward the door, when a loud knock without fell like the knell of hope upon their ears.

"My dear," screamed a shrill, angry, catamount-like voice through the key-hole, "are you inside there? I want to know, for here is Dominie Megapolensis waiting to see the poor young man that is to be hung. My de-e-e-e-r!"

A growling, inarticulate noise, issuing from the widely distended jaws of the jailer, manifested his attempt to reply to this invocation, and Jed, darting to his side with menacing gestures, crowded an ample handkerchief into his gulf-like mouth.

"He must be in there," continued the woman, apparently addressing some one at her side, after waiting in vain some moments for an answer: "he must be there, for the key is in the door inside; the lazy fellow has dropped asleep;" and this remark was followed by another screaming call, and a rattling of the door that might have awakened the seven sleepers of Ephesus.

In an agony of suspense, breathless and motionless, stood Jed and Rudolph, yet to the former returned at length a portion of the coolness and equanimity which had marked all his proceedings. Drawing his friend aside, he said, "Our only hope is in instant flight, for in three minutes this harridan will raise a mob. Keep perfectly still, and be guided by me, and if you get off, and we should be separated, remember that my hunter stands saddled just outside the wall, in the woods, about ten rods west of the centre gate—take this tarpaulin and spencer— do as I do, and be sure not to speak."

5

So saying, Jed doffed his jacket, exhibiting another exactly similar beneath it, and drew from his pocket a crushed cap like the one which he wore. "We are sailors,' he continued, "belonging to the Dolly, of and from Boston. Come on and keep calm, and, above all things, don't attempt to run, for the moonlight is like noonday without, and we shall be distinctly seen."

Resolving to be guided by one who had thus far shown so much sagacity and prudence, Rudolph followed his friend in silence to the door, which was still rattling in the vigorous grasp of Mrs. Gore. Obeying the gestures of Jed, he planted himself in a dark corner adjacent, while the former proceeded to turn the key, and confront the incensed matron whose voice was still heard without, mingling with the clatter of the shaken bars.

"Avast there, avast," he said, "can't you wait till the hatches are open, Mrs. Gore? There—come in now, if you want to—it isn't everybody that is so anxious to get in a place like this."

"What tom-foolery is all this, I should like to know?" said the vixen, bursting into the room, and followed more leisurely by the venerable and quiet clergyman; "what tom-foolery is this—and who are *you*—and where is that idiot of a Hugh Gore?"

"Your worthy husband sits yonder, madam," said Jed, "a little unwell, I believe," and the woman darted to her partner's side, while Jed, followed by Rudolph, stepped quickly out—and the clash of the closing door, and the sound of the turning lock, mingled with the shrill feminine scream that arose from within.

## CHAPTER XVIII.

Loud and louder rose the clamor from the jail, as, arm in arm, Jed and Rudolph descended the outer steps, and walked into the street; and ere they had gained the nearest corner, the stentorian voice of Hugh, rising like a thunder-tone above the shrill treble of his wife, told that all impediment to his speech had been removed. "Help—help—stop the murderers—fire—help," rang in every variety of tone and accent through the prison bars, until distant pedestrians paused to listen, and those more near hastened with a rush to the scene of the outcry.

"The whole street is alarmed," whispered Jed; "we must not run yet;" and then raising his voice, for numbers were passing them every instant, "The Dolly was nearly on her beam-ends, for it blew great guns, and the breakers wasn't more'n a cable's length off, when the captain came to me, and says, says he, Jack, says he——"

"Stop the murderers—stop the murderers!" came echoing down the street, and the clatter of coming feet was heard, and the bell of the old Dutch Church sent forth a rapid peal; but Jed and Rudolph still walked moderately forward.

"We must walk for a moment more," continued Jed in a whisper,—"the corner is close at hand—it would be fatal to run here," for the people were still hastening past them toward the jail, and eyeing curiously the two sailors, who, seeming so indifferent to the general commotion, were sauntering in an opposite direction.

"The truth is, the Dolly is a fine craft," he added in a louder tone, and Rudolph, looking up, saw Sinclair almost at his elbow passing with the crowd; "a little too square-built mayhap, and rather——"

The terrific voice of Hugh, sounding at this instant in their ears, told that the lion was unchained, and on their very path.

"Let some go to the river," he shouted, "and guard the boats, and others to the gates—quick, quick—we'll have them, my boys—they haven't got five minutes the start—stop the murderers—stop the murderers!" and the heavy footfall of Hugh echoed far and wide, as, with a long Indian-like lope, he went bounding through the street.

His voice fell upon the ears of the fugitives just as they had reached the corner of a road leading to the North River, and Jed, whispering "*Follow now*," dashed past his companion and led the race. Like the hunted herd they ran, but the pack, pursuing, open-mouthed and yelping, was on their track. The fugitives kept the riverward road until they came to an open field, or common, which stretched to the north, and across this, without any abatement of speed, they directed their course, keeping closely together. On emerging from the common they were compelled to cross a public road, beyond which lay another vacant field, reaching to the wall, which extended across the city from river to river, and formed its northern boundary. Apprehensive of being intercepted at this road, Jed and Rudolph took a circuit westward and crossed to the northern lot in safety, obtaining a view up the street as they passed which convinced them that the precaution had not been superfluous.

Three minutes more, and, panting with fatigue, they stood beside the wall, a dozen rods west of the gate, which, after pausing a moment for breath, they scaled with little difficulty, and caught sight of their pursuers not fifty yards behind. A shout of exultation from Hugh told that they in turn were perceived, and that their capture was regarded as certain. Jed paused for a moment, and a sickening fear came upon him as he looked vainly for his steed, but, at the next breath, a welcoming whinny from an adjoining copse told not only that his hunter was there, but that the faithful animal had recognized his master. Rushing to the spot, he disengaged him from a sapling to which he was fastened, and bade Rudolph mount and fly.

"Never, without you, Jed," exclaimed Groesbeck in a tone that forbade remonstrance; "I will not leave you in danger."

"*With* me then," returned the other, springing to the ample saddle as he spoke; "there is no time to parley."

Rudolph also mounted, and at the same instant a shout from the edge of the grove told that they were again perceived; but, answering to his master's voice, the faithful steed darted forward, and set all pursuit at defiance. Oaths and angry ejaculations attested the bitter disappointment of the jailer and his friends as they stood a moment later upon the deserted spot.

"It was a devilish deep-laid plot, whoever the fiend was that planned it," exclaimed Hugh, as he gazed after the flying steed; "but we must get horses and follow—they're not off the island yet by a long shot." So saying, he was about to return to the city, when a shout and commotion at a little distance arrested his attention.

"Here's one of 'em now—here's one of 'em," was the cry, as a dozen men darted into a thicket in chase of a retreating figure, and soon after emerged with the trembling tabernacle of poor old Jake, who had been keeping guard over the hunter, and had indiscreetly attempted to return before the rabble had dispersed. As his captors dragged the terrified slave from the cover of the woods into the moonlight, Hugh leaped with a shout of exultation toward him, but dreadful was his chagrin and wrath on perceiving the character of his prize.

"Who in the fiend's name are *you?*" he said, shaking the poor negro until his teeth rattled like a castanet. Trembling from head to foot, and utterly incapable of speech, Jake listened in silence to this adjuration, for being utterly unconscious of the object for which his services had been required by Jed, and unable in the confused state of his faculties to form a correct idea of any kind, he never doubted that he had fallen into the hands of some outlying band of savages, who were about to roast and eat him without ado.

"Who are you?" repeated Hugh in a towering rage, and again shaking his victim.

"Oh gor-a-massy," said the negro, holding on to his wool in momentary expectation of the scalping knife; "oh gor-a-massy, I don't know—I don't know."

A dozen hard cuffs on either side of his head did not appear in the least to enlighten the bewildered slave in regard to his identity, although they were doubtless bestowed with that amiable design; for he still persisted in saying, not without truth, that he did not know who he was. The jailer was not aware of the invulnerability of the African cranium, or of the very different locality to which flagellation should be applied on a negro in order to render it effectual. But poor Jake would have taken his beating more patiently if he had known how more precious than rubies, to his master and Rudolph, was every second of time which was thus employed. This thought occurred at length to Hugh, who, handing over the slave to some of his assistants to be preserved for future examination, hastened back to find means of prosecuting the chase.

Doleful beyond the power of language to depict was the little assembly which had convened on that memorable evening at the Bowery. But few comparatively of the confederates who, scarcely ten days before, had so joyously separated, sanguine with hope and expectation, were now assembled; for the consciousness of their utter inability to render any effectual assistance to Rudolph had deterred many from incurring personal hazard who otherwise would have been willing to risk much in his behalf. Confiscation and death were quite too formidable evils to be unnecessarily courted, and, although ever ready to respond to the call of patriotism or duty, their courage was not of that species which indulges in idle or boyish bravado.

Old Evert, who had sat long silent, with his hands and head resting upon his cane, rose with a heavy sigh, and walked across the floor; and the whisper went around that Rudolph and Effie were betrothed, and that Evert had only on that day learned it for the first, and that his daughter was even yet ignorant of her lover's danger. It was a melancholy scene, and tears sprang afresh to many an eye, when a sudden clatter of hoofs without, and a shout from the voice of Jed, brought the whole company in haste to the door.

"Give us fresh horses, for the love of Heaven!" he exclaimed. "Ceph is already blown, and the officers are close behind!"

None stopped to question, but rushing to the stables, the fleetest steeds were chosen and saddled in a breath—and scarce had their echoing feet died away in the distance before the sound of others approaching from the city was heard. So sudden and brief had been the interruption, and so intense the excitement, that scarcely any could believe it was a reality; but there was no time for gratulation, for prudence of course demanded the instant dissolution of a conclave which might so naturally create suspicion as to its design. With hasty adieus the guests departed by a retired road, and by the time Hugh and his train had reached the governor's house all was quiet; even Bucephalus, Jed's discarded steed, having been removed into an adjoining wood, lest his presence might betray his master's agency in the rescue. It may be deemed no reasonable cause of surprise, that while the main body of the pursuers pressed hotly forward on the highway, a portion of them stopped to search the premises of the ex-governor. Yet not a little amazed did Stuyvesant seem at the Goth-like irruption into his domicile, where he was found quietly smoking his pipe, and reading with great interest an Amsterdam gazette, some eighteen months old, which he had long known by heart. Feigning the wrath which his ecstasy of joy would not allow him to feel, he beheld the myrmidons of the law overrunning his house from cellar to attic, fierce as hounds seeking to unearth their prey; and many were the unintelligible taunts which he safely showered upon them in Low Dutch, while following them up from room to room. On their sudden departure also he blazed forth a "fire in their rear" of double chain-shot anathemas, which, although formidable to hear, is believed to have produced no fatal effects.

Whoever had seen the broad, fat, laughing face that re-entered Governor Stuyvesant's house to the double quick-step music of a lignum-vitæ leg, might have believed that he had encountered the original Comus, grown old and crippled. Thump, thump, thump, rang the heavy blows across the echoing floor, as, scarcely assisted by his cane, he walked rapidly to and fro in a whirlwind of joyous excitement.

"They'll never catch my grays," he said; "never, never; they might as well chase the wind; Ru and Jed will be at Devil Creek in half an hour, and from there they will soon reach a place of safety in the wilderness. They'll never catch my Donner and Blitzen—never—never!"

Let it suffice for the present to say that the venerable Peter had not overpraised his steeds, or miscalculated results; for long before daylight the discomfited pursuers returned, utterly baffled in their search. They had entirely lost track of the fugitives, being unable to learn at what point they had crossed the shallow creek which bounds the island on the north. That they had found shelter somewhere in the boundless wilderness which stretched interminably northward was the only fact, galling, scathing, rage-inciting, which they were able to bear back to their awfully incensed governor, Sir Francis Lovelace.

Old Jake meanwhile was in prison, in full view of the gallows, and in the firmest possible faith that his unfortunate body was destined to be framed therein with all reasonable dispatch. He had been confined to await the leisure of his captors, who felt certain of thus possessing a direct clew to the mysterious agent in the rescue of Rudolph. He was honored accordingly on the ensuing morning by a visit from the governor in person, accompanied by the crest-fallen but still scowling jailer, and no small train beside.

Fully impressed with the belief that he was to be led to instant execution, the negro went darting like a madman about the room, diving into all imaginable nooks and corners to evade his supposed pursuers; and it was only after much delay and parley that he could be made to comprehend what was really wanted of him. But the whole story was at length elicited, and great was the astonishment and indignation of Lovelace and his retainers on learning that it was the young Knickerbocker who had thus wrested their victim from their hands, and brought disgrace and ridicule upon the government. While the examination was pending, Hugh, who stood a little apart from the rest of the company, and apparently quite inattentive to the proceedings, was diligently engaged in arranging a sliding noose to a stout hempen cord.

"When is it your excellency's pleasure that it shall be done?" he said, addressing the governor as the latter was about to withdraw.

" What, Hugh—what? do you want to hang the negro?"

" Why, yes," said Hugh, " I suppose he is to be turned off, of course ; it may as well be now as at any other time ; everything is ready, and it is certainly very clear from his own confessions that he assisted in the escape."

"But he hasn't been tried, Hugh, or sentenced," said the governor, apparently in doubt, and looking very earnestly in the jailer's face.

" Wal, I suppose that can be done afterwards just as well," answered Hugh, playing with the rope—" or for that matter, here is a full Court present—your honor and Justices Smith and Clark ; you've heern his confessions, and now you can sentence him."

" Very true—very true," said the governor, while the negro, pale with fright, his teeth audibly chattering, stood staring, speechless, at him. " What say you, brethren of the bench?— my opinion is that the negro is guilty of aiding in the forcible rescue of Rudolph Groesbeck, a convicted traitor——"

Hugh stretched his rope, and made more sure of the knot——

—— " and my sentence is that he be discharged without further punishment. He acted under his master's orders," said Lovelace, opening the door, " and knew nothing of the foul crime which he was abetting—scamper home, you black dog;" and Jake, darting through the doorway, went bounding through the streets like a madman, looking ever and anon behind him, to see if he was pursued.

" It shall never be said," continued Lovelace, "that we wreaked our vengeance on a brainless slave; and now, my friends, we will see what steps can be taken for the recapture of our prisoner, and his very valorous friend, for that we shall have them yet, you may be well assured."

So saying, the governor and his attendants withdrew, and Mr. Hugh Gore, scowling not a little, hung his hempen necklace on a nail, and wondered very much whether he should ever really have the pleasure of adjusting it under the ears of any human being. More especially and more longingly did he wonder whether he should ever be able to pay so delicate a mark of attention to that very jovial gentleman who had treated him to such liberal draughts of Mr. Huyck's genuine Jamaica.

## CHAPTER XIX.

THE danger was not past. Grateful as had been the sense of relief experienced by Rudolph's friends at his escape, they could not but feel that his situation was still one of extreme hazard, and that another of their number, equally worthy, had now become involved in the peril. Outlawed men, co-tenants with the savage of a barren wilderness, with no accessible resort in civilized life, which was not under the jurisdiction of the government they had offended, what hope was there for them of surviving the perils to which they were exposed? That Lovelace would not for an hour intermit his efforts for their capture, there was every reason to believe. Rumors of his contemplated movements came continually to their ears, and it soon became certain that a company of horsemen were to be sent out to scour the forest in every direction. These it was thought could not fail of success; and having returned triumphant, the affront which had been offered to the majesty of the law was to be expiated by a double sacrifice.

But the Dutch citizens meanwhile were not idle. Scarcely an hour elapsed on the day following the escape, in which some horsemen might not be seen travelling northward, slowly and quietly at first, but outstripping the wind when the forest road was gained. These, bearing provisions for the temporary sustenance of their friends, hoped to discover their retreat, and be enabled not only to administer to their wants, but to keep them advised of the movements of their enemies. But friend and foe were alike unsuccessful in their efforts, and three days of futile search had elapsed when tidings of a new device on the part of the officials of the law diffused terror among the opposite party.

Indian scouts or runners were to be sent out who could tread the mazy forests with ease, and follow the trail of the light-footed deer across the pathless wilds; and these were to be accompanied by armed men in sufficient numbers to make sure of the capture of the fugitives. There were no Indians who, properly speaking, sojourned in the city, but there was a class of this people, erratic as comets, who emerged at irregular intervals from the wilderness, and, passing a few days as hangers-

5*

on at the fort, and in the vicinity of those shops where the enticing fire-water was to be procured, departed again as suddenly as they had appeared.

Among these was one known as the Raven, a noted runner or news carrier among the tribes; who was famous also for his accuracy in following a trail, however carefully it had been concealed. His reputation in these matters was founded on the concurrent testimony of many of his red brethren, none of whom pretended to compete with him in these qualities. But the Raven was at this time absent from town, and as his motions, governed by unknown laws, were too eccentric to admit of being calculated, particularly when subjected to certain disturbing influences, bottled and corked, which he usually carried with him from the city, it became necessary first to send a messenger of more humble pretensions in quest of him.

One of his own people was accordingly dispatched to bring him in, and in the mean time every preparation was made for the expedition, which it was believed could not fail of success. The anxiety of the friends of the young men greatly increased, and, being themselves closely watched on all sides, it became difficult even to concert any countervailing action, much more to carry it into effect. Evert, from an ecstasy of joy, had sunk again into utter despondency, and was haunted continually by visions of his son and Rudolph perishing in the forests or dragged as prisoners to the city; while Effie, who had been informed of all the circumstances on the evening of the flight, was tossed by those tumultuous emotions of hope and fear, which, racking the soul with agony, forbade any distinct perception of realities.

It was in this state of mind that, on the afternoon of the fourth day succeeding the escape, she resorted alone, as was then frequently her custom, to a small observatory on the housetop. From this prominent post of observation she surveyed the road which led northward from the city, and gazing far away toward those boundless forests, which, somewhere within their depths, sheltered her exiled friends, she reflected with anguish on the pains and perils to which they were exposed.

But when, from the frowning forests, her gaze ascended to the blue summer sky which was bending tranquilly above them, her tortured breast became more calm; for then she remembered her accustomed reliance, in every strait, on that Infinite Power and Beneficence which saves alike "by many or by few."

Again changing her field of view, she gazed down the bay, which was slightly ruffled by a southern breeze, and her eyes rested upon the distant point where the converging shores leave but a narrow outlet to that wider expanse of waters known as the lower bay.

Was it a cloud that hung midway between the shores, and moved slowly toward the north? Another followed in the distance, and yet another was turning the furthermost point of land; and now she perceives distinctly, as she shades her eyes with her hands and looks more closely, that they are not clouds, but vessels with their sails spread, coming in from sea, and that two more have been added to the number. So rare an occurrence could not fail to excite surprise, and Effie hastened to inform her father, who was sitting in his accustomed corner of the stoop below.

"Five vessels in the Narrows, standing up the bay, do you say?" asked the old man, trembling as he rose, and looking with almost maniacal wildness at his daughter.

"Yes, papa," said Effie; "you can see them distinctly from the house-top."

"God of Heaven!" exclaimed Evert reverentially, clasping his hands and looking upward, "thou hast sent us aid at last."

"Papa—dear papa!" screamed Effie, clinging to him with sudden alarm; "what is it that you mean?"

"*It is the Dutch fleet, my child,*" exclaimed Evert, springing to the stairway with the step of a youth; "it is the Dutch fleet, and it has come to save us all from ruin."

Climbing with agility to the roof, the old man dashed the blinding tears from his eyes, and, gazing earnestly down the bay, saw a glorious confirmation of his hopes. The ships had passed the Narrows and were coming up under flowing sail toward the city; and while he trembled lest there should be some mistake, the voice of Effie was again heard calling from below:

"Papa, O papa—here comes young Harmon Van Rensselaer riding furiously down the street; his horse is covered with foam, and he is swinging his hat in the air; he comes this way, papa, directly toward our house;" and by the time that Evert had again reached the piazza, the equestrian was galloping down the lawn.

"*A fleet—a fleet from home!*" he shouted, pausing but a breath, and pointing down the bay; "I have seen the colors of the States at their masts;" and turning his steed, his flushed face vanished as suddenly as it had appeared, and the clattering of his horse's hoofs was heard as he hastened to diffuse the tidings, and his echoing voice came back as he shouted to some passing friend, "*A fleet—a fleet from home!*"

Like the Highland henchman, with his cross of fire, speeding to call his clan to arms, the young Van Rensselaer, heedless of danger, and exulting in the glorious intelligence which he bore, passed from house to house spreading the news among the principal Dutch inhabitants of this city; and then turning his panting steed northward, he went dashing toward the Bowery. Governor Stuyvesant was sitting on his stoop, giving directions from time to time to the slow-witted Hans, who, *tête-à-tête*, with a row of promising cabbage-heads in the adjoining garden, was tending and cultivating them with a sort of fraternal solicitude.

"What madman comes here?" he exclaimed, as Harmon came galloping up; "put a beggar on horseback, and he'll ride to——"

"Huzza! huzza! huzza!" shouted Van Rensselaer, leaping from his steed, and swinging his cap as he rushed on the stoop, and seizing and shaking both the old man's hands at once. "There is a Dutch fleet standing up the bay with all sails set," he said; "in three hours New York will again belong to Holland."

"Are you sure, Harmon?" asked the governor energetically, when after several seconds he found voice to reply; "are you quite sure that this glorious news is true?"

A booming gun at this moment, reverberating through the air, seemed to answer the inquiry; another and another followed in quick succession.

"They are themselves announcing their approach," said Harmon rapidly · "there is, there can be no mistake; I myself have seen the colors of the States, floating from the masts—huzza! huzza!" and Stuyvesant joined vociferously in the shouts of his young companion, swinging his cane meanwhile over his head, and making the whole house resound with the clatter of his wooden leg. Hans next added his hoarse voice to the concert, and a rushing concourse of negroes, springing as if by magic from every quarter, soon joined in the deafening cheers. Doors and windows flew open, and the whole household of the governor came pouring out to learn the cause of the uproar, and finally to join heartily in the merriment. The frightened fowls fled cackling in every direction—the dogs turned their noses up into the air, and barked knowingly toward the chimneys; and in the midst of the uproar, the sound of wheels was heard—first from one direction and then from another, and the Van Schaicks and Van Tines, and Van Pelts, and Van Dams, came pouring in and adding their shouts and exultations to the tumult.

In ten minutes the whole of that band of confederates who had been present on the night of Rudolph's dangerous commission were reassembled, with many more beside. The most hearty congratulations were exchanged on all sides, and nothing was seen but shaking of hands and nodding of heads, and nothing heard but a Babel-like jargon resounding on every side, interspersed with noisy laughter and every token of delight. The

hubbub of a New England town meeting, or the din of a fourfold
auction in the reverberating rotunda of the modern Exchange,
may serve in some degree to illustrate the uproar.

But the turmoil subsided at length, and the assembly resolved
itself in a sort of informal council, or what in more modern par-
lance might perhaps be termed a provisional government, with a
view to take any necessary measures for a general co-operation
with their foreign friends. Various expedients were proposed,
but the upshot of the deliberations was, that every man should
hasten home, and, arming himself and his slaves, stand ready
for such emergencies as should arise. A committee of vigilance
was appointed, and Major Ver Planck was put in command of
the forces.

"We'll get retty, my friends," said the Major; "but ef there
are five sheeps-of-war there won't be mooch for us to do—they'll
batter down the fort, and all three of the redoubts, and half the
town besides, in ten minutes—but then we'll get retty, my friends
—we'll get retty."

The next thing in order was to transmit intelligence of these
events, if possible, to Rudolph and Jed, and it was resolved to
send messengers immediately in every direction in pursuit of
them. A dozen young men at once volunteered on this service, pledging themselves to explore the forests for a week,
rather than return without success. The Raven had not yet
made his appearance, and it was confidently believed that he
could be intercepted, and made to serve their own purposes,
inasmuch as the intended governmental expedition would doubtless be at once abandoned. If he could not be found, however,
it was hoped that other similar agents could be procured in the
wilderness, and, full of confident anticipation, the little party of
cavalry set out on their expedition on that very evening. The
party meanwhile had dispersed, Mr. Knickerbocker only remaining to smoke a pipe with his friend, and quaff a bumper of genuine Hollands to the thrice glorious event which was yet too
full of dazzling hope to be contemplated with any degree of
equanimity.

Of the events which ensued on that very memorable thirtieth
of July, in the year of grace 1673, the historical reader needs
scarcely to be informed. The fleet came to anchor at a considerable distance below the city, and on that same evening Colonel
Manning, the commandant of the fort, impelled doubtless by a
sense of its indefensible condition, sent down the keys to the
Dutch admirals; an act for which he was subsequently tried
by court-martial, and degraded, but escaped severer punishment.

But what language shall describe the scenes of the ensuing
morning, when the hundreds of sleepless eyes which had " out-

watched the stars," waiting for the momentous events of the
coming day, were greeted at dawn with the sight of their native
flag floating in triumph from every corner of the fort. The
work was accomplished. The mighty achievement of which
they had talked, and thought, and dreamed for nine long years,
was wrought as if by magic before their eyes; and the New
Netherlands were once more a province of Holland. Of the
details of the capitulation, and of the surrender of the forts of
Albany and on the Delaware, which soon after ensued, it is unnecessary to speak. Let it suffice to say that the re-conquest
was thorough, complete, and undisputed.

## CHAPTER XX.

THE admirals and captains of the victorious fleet held a council on shipboard before disembarking, for the purpose of appointing a governor to the province, having been thereto empowered by the home government; and it having been ascertained that Stuyvesant, by reason of his age and infirmities, preferred not to be recalled to that post, the dignity was devolved upon one of their own number, Captain Andrew Colve. The new governor, the admirals, and other officers of the fleet, assembled on the same afternoon, by invitation, at the house of Mr. Knicker-bocker, where they were met by the principal Dutch inhabitants of the city. Here a scene of unrestrained hilarity ensued, in which, without any undue exultation over their adversaries, every one gave free scope to his exuberant joy. There were a multitude of matters to be discussed, pertaining both to the expedition and the taking of the city, and also to the state of the pending war in Europe; and as the party, to the number of fifty or sixty, were divided into little knots of six or eight, in each of which there were at least two talkers to one listener, it will be believed that a very respectable amount of colloquial power was kept in operation.

The governor, ex-governor Stuyvesant, and the two admirals, of course received a more respectful hearing than others, but joy, like grief, is a great leveller, and there was no very marked deference to rank exacted or bestowed. Indeed, there came a time before the evening passed away, in which a considerable degree of confusion must have resulted from any attempt to establish rights of precedence; Governor Colve having been heard to address a second lieutenant by the title of admiral, and the venerable Stuyvesant making some earnest inquiries when the attack on the fort was to commence, as he had put Yawpy Poffenburgh in command of the forces, and they were all ready to march.

If, however, any such little aberrations occurred, it was at a late hour in the evening, when people grow sleepy and naturally make mistakes. There was, it is true, a very large punch-bowl standing on the sideboard, cheek by jowl with a pitcher of spiced toddy, and now and then a decanter of the raw material, and the fumes which arose from these sources may possibly have had something to do with the matter.

But this is getting altogether ahead of the story. It was at an earlier hour, and long before sunset, that the supper-table was set out on the long piazza, for there was no room in the house competent for such a purpose, and if there had been, there could have been none half as pleasant. The fresh air from the river circulated freely through the porch, while the large shade-trees adjacent excluded the sun, and gave shelter to a band of feathered musicians, which, flitting briskly about, kept up a sort of chirruping chorus to the shouts and laughter that arose from within. As the superintendence of this momentous part of the entertainment had been committed to Effie, her sense of responsibility was a very weighty one, and probably not materially inferior to that of Governor Colve on taking his new command.

But dear Effie had the assistance of the family slaves, and of six borrowed ones beside, in addition to which a row of amateurs, to the number of fifteen or twenty, decorated the outside of the piazza, looking on with every demonstration of delight which owl-like eyes and white teeth could give, and ready to render any extra assistance that might be required. Indeed, any manifestation of a desire for their aid was apt to be followed by a struggle for the honor of rendering it, which created no slight disturbance; but the good feeling was too general to allow of any censure being bestowed for such a cause.

Although Effie's joy, like that of her father, was materially moderated by her fears for Rudolph and Jed, yet the spirit of hope predominated; for the measures which had been taken for the discovery of the young men, it was believed, could scarcely fail of success. It was a sumptuous repast, around which, at a summons from Jake, now transformed into head butler, the happy party gathered, and remained standing, while Dominie Megapolensis, his white locks resting on his shoulders, invoked a blessing from above. The rich and savory dishes which sent up their flavor from every side were not a little grateful to the senses of men who were not accustomed to slight the creature comforts of life; and more especially to that portion of them, who for months preceding had been restricted to the coarser fare incident to a life at sea.

How gloatingly did their eyes fall upon the dishes of roasted and stewed, and broiled and baked, which were scattered in profusion on every side; the tender juicy steaks, drowned in gravy; the huge tureens of oysters; the rashers of bacon and new-laid eggs, the roasted ducks, and roasted chickens, and roasted geese; the *saurkraut*, and *kohlslaa*, and *simaa* and *rulliches*;

to say nothing of a side table laden with pies and puddings, and a perfect Himmaleh of doughnuts; and with the many-twisted, crisp, crumbling crullers, which were made on principle so that every part should be of just the thickness of Effie's little finger. The beverage of tea was unknown at that period in this country, and formed of course no part of the repast, but, as has been already hinted, there was no lack of certain other potables, which in those dark ages were deemed reasonably palatable. Conversation sank to a very low ebb for a while, being superseded by the clatter of knives and forks, and by the occasional clash of conflicting waiters, one of whom, being lost in admiration of Admiral Evertsen's golden sword-hilt, deposited a dish of oyster-soup in the ample lap of an adjoining burgher.

But the meal was nearly ended, and the guests had begun to eat more leisurely, and Governor Stuyvesant's man Hans, who was inseparable from his master, and who had been sitting for the last hour in a quiet corner of the stoop, in a dozing, half-dreamy state, now begun to calculate at each waking how near his own chance at the tempting viands had approached. And the waiters within, and the waiters without, knowing full well that they would be stinted in none of the luxuries on which their eyes had long been feasting, were making similar calculations as to time, and chuckling at each sign of a guest giving out. But Hans has awakened more fully than usual; he has even opened his lips in that august presence; he has raised his hand—he speaks, he gesticulates, and the outsiders are stricken dumb at his audacity.

"Hark!" said Hans, raising his forefinger, and all eyes were turned toward him, Governor Stuyvesant frowning not a little.

"Hark!" he repeated, still elevating his hand.

"What does the idiot mean?" asked Stuyvesant, angrily; "what do you hear, boy?"

"It's Donner and Blitzen!" said the lad; "*I* know their gallop!"

A slight scream arose from Effie;—Evert and Stuyvesant, with half of the guests, sprang to their feet, and rushed out on the lawn, while the naval officers, ignorant at first of what was meant, looked on in utter amazement. Hans was not deceived. In two minutes Jed and Rudolph were in the arms of their friends, pulled and hauled on every side, thronged and pressed, and climbed upon, and held by the hands, and by the arms, and by the shoulders, and questioned with thirty questions at once, and informed by thirty voices of what they already knew, that New York was reconquered, and that they were both safe from the gibbet, and that the great admirals and the new governor were all then and there present.

The paternal eye of Evert was the first to perceive that the young men were suffering severely from fatigue and famine, and that no kindness would be as appreciable by them as food and repose. They were therefore suffered, after a formal presentation to the strangers, to withdraw to another room, promising to rejoin the company in the course of the evening. Effie had vanished from the party at the first alarm, and to her, as may well be supposed, the first thoughts of the new-comers were directed. They met at once; it was a voiceless interview at first, in which tears that could not be repressed told of feelings that could not be uttered. Pale, hollow-cheeked, and travel-stained, the fainting young men sank exhausted into seats, and gave way to feelings which a greater degree of strength would have enabled them to restrain.

But a little repose, and a little speedy refreshment, and the cheering voice of Effie, who flew bustling in every direction to administer to their wants, acted like a charm upon the sufferers, and at the end of an hour Jed was sufficiently restored to rejoin his father's guests. Not so, however, with Rudolph, who did not deem it safe to abandon his medical adviser until a much later period. When he did so, however, the renewed sparkling of his eye, and a general vivacity of manner, gave token of some change of treatment which had proved highly favorable to his case.

On joining the company, he found himself, moreover, at once transformed into a lion of very formidable dimensions—a very Lybian, both in roar and mane.

He was not prepared for the congratulations which poured in upon him from all sides, and much less for being told by the gallant Admiral Evertsen that his patriotic services, his self-devoting heroism, and his near approach to martyrdom, should not only be duly represented at home, but that they would not be overlooked by the new colonial government.

When the excitement occasioned by Rudolph's entrance had somewhat subsided, and conversation had again become general, Governor Stuyvesant, whose countenance had long given token of some earnest purpose, rose with much emotion to propose a toast. The anxious and inquiring look which he gave at the same time to the admirals and the new governor, evinced that it was not without some degree of trepidation and doubt that he spoke. A general silence prevailed, and all eyes were fixed wonderingly on the speaker, when, raising his brimming glass, he said, "I give you—

"*Justice to Evert Knickerbocker!*"

There was a moment of painful doubt; for, although all present were familiar with the history of Evert's wrongs, the former apathy of the home government on the subject had created fears that even now, when it was so easy to award restitution, the new governor might be backward about doing so. The suspense, however, lasted but a moment. No sooner had Admiral Evertsen fully comprehended the meaning of the toast, than, elevating his glass, he repeated it in an emphatic voice; Benckes and Colve did the same, and the words, "Justice to Evert Knickerbocker," resounded in a hearty chorus from every part of the table, followed by a clinking of glasses, and a hearty "three times three," led off by Governor Colve himself. At the next moment Evert's friends crowded around him with hearty congratulations, while the old man, taken entirely by surprise, was able only with tears and disjointed words to express his emotions.

The party dispersed at a late hour, in merry mood, and on the next day Mr. Knickerbocker received a valid patent for the whole length and breadth of those very domains which sixteen years before had been voted to him in council. Whether the claims of the heirs of Sharp would under other circumstances have been at all considered, may be a matter of conjecture; but the abduction of Hiram, and the uncertainty whether he was in existence or not, had made it impossible for Lovelace to issue a patent either to him or his children; and the title had been withheld to await some settlement, either by lapse of time or otherwise, of that question. The title to the other two-thirds had also remained in the English government, and the whole thus passing by reconquest to the new sovereignty, there was nothing in the way of awarding the most full and complete restitution. It was done, and Evert did not neglect, this time, either the recording of his deed, or the subsequent safe disposition of the original document.

## CHAPTER XXI.

On that memorable day which beheld the re-transfer of the province of New York to the Dutch, Mr. Benhadad Sharp was absent from the city, being engaged on his estates, renewing some expired leases, and grinding the faces of some very poor and very industrious tenants.

"Never since I have been a——a patroon," said Benhadad to himself, assuming a title which he had long coveted; "never since I have been a patroon," he said, as he journeyed leisurely homeward, "did I see such indolence and neglect; and they to prate about agues and fevers, and their troops of children to be fed and clothed, the little dirty ragamuffins! but they'll find there's to be a change: I've raised on 'em all round, enough to make a hundred pounds extra in my pocket for the next year, and I shall tell the governor to do the same. I'm harder than Mr. Knickerbocker, am I, Mr. Simpkins?—very well, I'll be harder still next year; I'll have no lazy whining fellows about me;" for Simpkins and Schmidt and Thompson, who had swarms of youngsters, had all told the young landlord how Evert had always thrown off something of his dues from them on account of their children; "I'm harder, am I?" continued the soliloquist; "very well—I'll be harder still, and teach you better manners—I'll——"

Bang! bang! bang! came the sound of the cannon up the bay, echoing far and wide across the silent waters, and over the distant hills: for it was evening, and the admirals had just received the keys off Staten Island, as has been related in the preceding chapter.

"What in the name of wonder does all that mean?" continued Sharp, who had now reached the ferry boat, a huge scow, pulled by ropes across the river, at its narrowest part; "what's all that firing at the fort, Mr. Schnipper?"

"'Tain't at the fort, that ain't, Mr. Sharp, by no manner of means," said the ferryman, who, being a Dutchman, was chuckling delightedly as he spoke; "it's the Dutch, sir, that is—the

Dutch, sir—sixteen men-of-war, which are going to take the city at daybreak to-morrow mornin'—that's all."

There are no words in any human vocabulary to express Benhadad's astonishment and alarm, for, obtuse as he was on many points, he was remarkably clear-sighted in whatever pertained to his own pecuniary interest, and he foresaw at once the whole probable sequence of events in relation to the Knickerbocker manor. How great was his cause for grief will be better understood when it is said, that, in a formal division with his sister of their patrimony, he had accepted the manor lands as his half, felicitating himself not a little on having obtained the lion's share. That no re-division could be hoped for, had been rendered quite certain by another singular event which had occurred a short time prior, being nothing less than the sudden marriage of Euphemia to one Charles Augustus Sinclair, late a captain in the Spanish naval service. Benhadad did not reply to the ferryman, and was aroused from his painful reverie only by being notified that the boat was ready.

But if the boat was ready, the traveller was not. Visions of a tremendous bombardment—of red-hot shells flying through the air—of a desperate encounter under the walls of the fort, began to take possession of his mind, and inasmuch as fighting was quite against his principles, he resolved to return to his estate, and there await the expected thunderbolt which was to shatter his fortunes. If this anticipation was not a very pleasing one, it was at least of no long continuance; for in forty-eight hours Mr. Knickerbocker was in person on the estate, fully reinstated in his rights, and receiving the congratulations of his thronging tenantry.

The new government did not stop midway in its measures, "We must give Rudolph a potato-patch," said Colve to his councillors at one of their earliest sittings, running his finger meanwhile over a number of unappropriated townships on a map which was spread out before him, and finally selecting one containing about four square miles, in the neighborhood of the Knickerbocker manor. "That will do," he said; "what say you, gentlemen,—has Rudolph Groesbeck deserved such a mark of his country's gratitude?" A unanimous voice approved the governor's liberality, and the grant was immediately made.

It required time to appreciate the magical change which had been so suddenly wrought in the fortunes of the Knickerbockers, and of Rudolph. Their indigence had been changed to affluence, their danger to security, their distress to happiness, and no trace of departed griefs remained, excepting that remembrance of their existence, which serves to heighten the enjoyment of present prosperity. Many were the subsequent scenes of hilarity which ensued at the old homestead; but the earliest and most prominent of these was one which will be too easily imagined to require any detailed description.

Evert's house was one of ample dimensions, but it was for once filled to overflowing; for old and young were there, graybearded men, and ancient matrons, blooming belles and dashing beaux, and even wee children, to attend the mystical ceremony by which Rudolph and Effie were to be united in perpetual league. It was the season of flowers, and the bride, in accordance with the simple tastes of the age, was adorned with a roseate diadem, which, however much a decoration, manifestly received more lustre than it imparted. Rudolph's commanding figure, the joyous Jed, the venerable Evert, with Stuyvesant and Colve and old Dominie Megapolensis, erect and stately, were among the conspicuous features of the assemblage. The crowded room, the open windows thronged on the outer side by guests who could not get in, the tier of slaves still further removed, and peering, with sable necks outstretched, from the tops of adjacent railings and fences, presented altogether a picture of delight and satisfaction, not often seen or easily forgotten.

The merry-making which followed the ceremony was free and unrestrained and lasted untill a late hour in the evening: the pillars of the long piazza being made to shake by the hour to the tread of the twenty-four couple of contra-dancers, who responded to the violent and tugging efforts of three African fiddlers, perched on an eminence just without the porch. As there was nothing to mar the pleasures of the evening, so did these prove a significant prelude to the long after years of harmony and happiness, which marked the lot of the newly wedded.

Jed continued his woodland sports, until diverted from the chase by a new variety of game in the pursuit of which he exhibited his usual skill and success. In other words, he soon brought home a gentle bride; but the friends whom adversity had united, prosperity did not separate. In that ancient homestead, rendered sacred by its connection with the marked events of the past, they all resided together for many happy years.

Evert lived to an advanced age, and smoked a thousand peaceful pipes in his favorite corner of the stoop, slightly disturbed perhaps, at times, by the shouts of noisy children on the green, who called him by a new and welcome name. Upspringing like roses about his path, these became the light of his eyes, and the core of his heart. The morning and the eve of life—how strongly do they contrast, and yet how harmoniously do they blend; the innocence of childhood, and the piety of guileless age, alike eliciting the smiles and protection of that Infinite Beneficence whose purity they reflect.

Governor Stuyvesant lived also to a ripe age, and, like Evert, in the enjoyment of serene and tranquil days, scarcely disturbed even by the subsequent cession of the province to England by the Dutch, which occurred at the close of the war between those nations. He died in August, 1682, and an ancient slab of free-stone, still to be seen against the base of St. Mark's church in the modern metropolis, indicates the place of his repose. There are gorgeous monuments to his more wealthy descendants within the edifice, but the old, gray, weather-beaten stone without, alone proclaims the resting-place of the illustrious founder of the family.

Lovelace was ordered to depart from the province, and Egbert Groesbeck, bankrupt in purse and in reputation, was among those who joined the train of the ex-governor, and went to England. He did not scruple, however, to receive a liberal present from his brother on the eve of departure, or to suggest the address to which any similar mark of favor might be forwarded.

As neither Ripley nor Sharp was ever heard of again, it is supposed that the former concluded to throw off his allegiance to Sinclair, and take the destinies of the Zephyr and its prisoner into his own hands, in which event the fate of the latter may readily be conjectured.

The means by which Captain Sinclair had succeeded in supplanting his friend in the affections of Euphemia were not altogether apparent, but it soon became evident that the latter had no very strong hold upon her volatile and jovial partner. He soon began to manifest a singular propensity to transmute his property of every description into bullion, and, with the exception of a small estate which had fortunately been settled upon his wife, accomplished his purpose, although of course at a great sacrifice. Soon afterwards he received some important intelligence from Spain, which demanded his presence in that country for a few months, whither he accordingly departed, taking care to carry his gold along with him. Singularly enough, however, the Captain neglected to return to America, and it was supposed that he had been prevailed upon to remain abroad by the urgent entreaties of his many distinguished friends, the Count Sylvio not excepted.

THE END.